PAPERCUTZ SLICES

PERCY JERKSON

& THE OVOLACTOVEGETARIANS

YOU'LL NEVER DIGEST ME, NEVER! THERE'S A LITTLE McKRONOS IN EVERYONE... FOREVER!
MWHAHAHAHA!
AND SO, AN EXTRA LARGE VALUE THREAT WAS UNLEASHED...

PAPERCUTZ

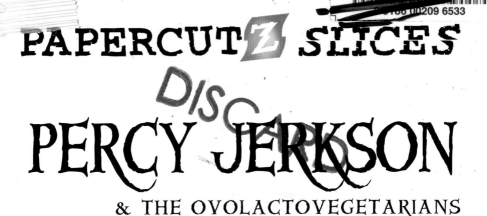

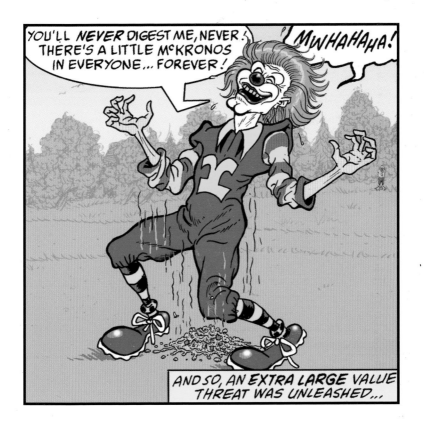

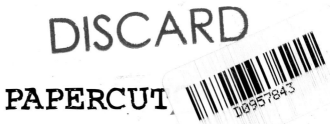

PAPERCUTZ SLICES

Graphic Novels Available from PAPERCUTZ (Who else..?!)

Graphic Novel #1
"Harry Potty and
the Deathly Boring"

Graphic Novel #2
"Breaking Down"

Graphic Novel #3
"Percy Jerkson & The
Ovolactovegetarians"

PAPERCUTZ SLICES graphic novels are available at booksellers everywhere. At bookstores, comicbook stores, online, out of the trunk in the back of Rick Parker's car, and who knows where else? If you still are unable to find PAPERCUTZ SLICES (probably because it sold out) you can always order directly from Papercutz—but it'll cost you! PAPERCUTZ SLICES is available in paperback for $6.99 each; in hardcover for $10.99 each. But that's not the worst part-- please add $4.00 for postage and handling for the first book, and add $1.00 for each additional book. Going to your favorite bookseller, buying online, or even getting a copy from your local library doesn't seem so bad now, does it? But if you still insist on ordering from Papercutz, and just to make everything just a little bit more complicated, please make your check payable to NBM Publishing. Don't ask why—it's just how it works. Send to: Papercutz, 40 Exchange Place, Ste. 1308, New York, NY 10005 Or call 800 886 1223 (9-6 EST M-F) MC-Visa-Amex accepted

www.papercutz.com

PAPERCUTZ SLICES

#3 PERCY JERKSON

& THE OVOLACTOVEGETARIANS

MARGO KINNEY-PETRUCHA & STEFAN PETRUCHA
Writers
RICK PARKER
Artist

New York

"PERCY JERKSON & THE OVOLACTOVEGETARIANS"

MARGO KINNEY-PETRUCHA & STEFAN PETRUCHA – Writers
RICK PARKER – Artist
RICK PARKER – Colorist
RICK PARKER – Letterer

SHELLY STERNER & CHRIS NELSON
Production

MICHAEL PETRANEK
Associate Editor

JIM SALICRUP
Editor-in-Chief

ISBN: 978-1-59707-264-9 paperback edition
ISBN: 978-1-59707-265-6 hardcover edition

Printed in China
August 2011 by New Era Printing, LTD
Trend Centre, 29-31 Cheung Lee St.
Chaiwan, Hong Kong

First Printing
Distributed by Macmillan

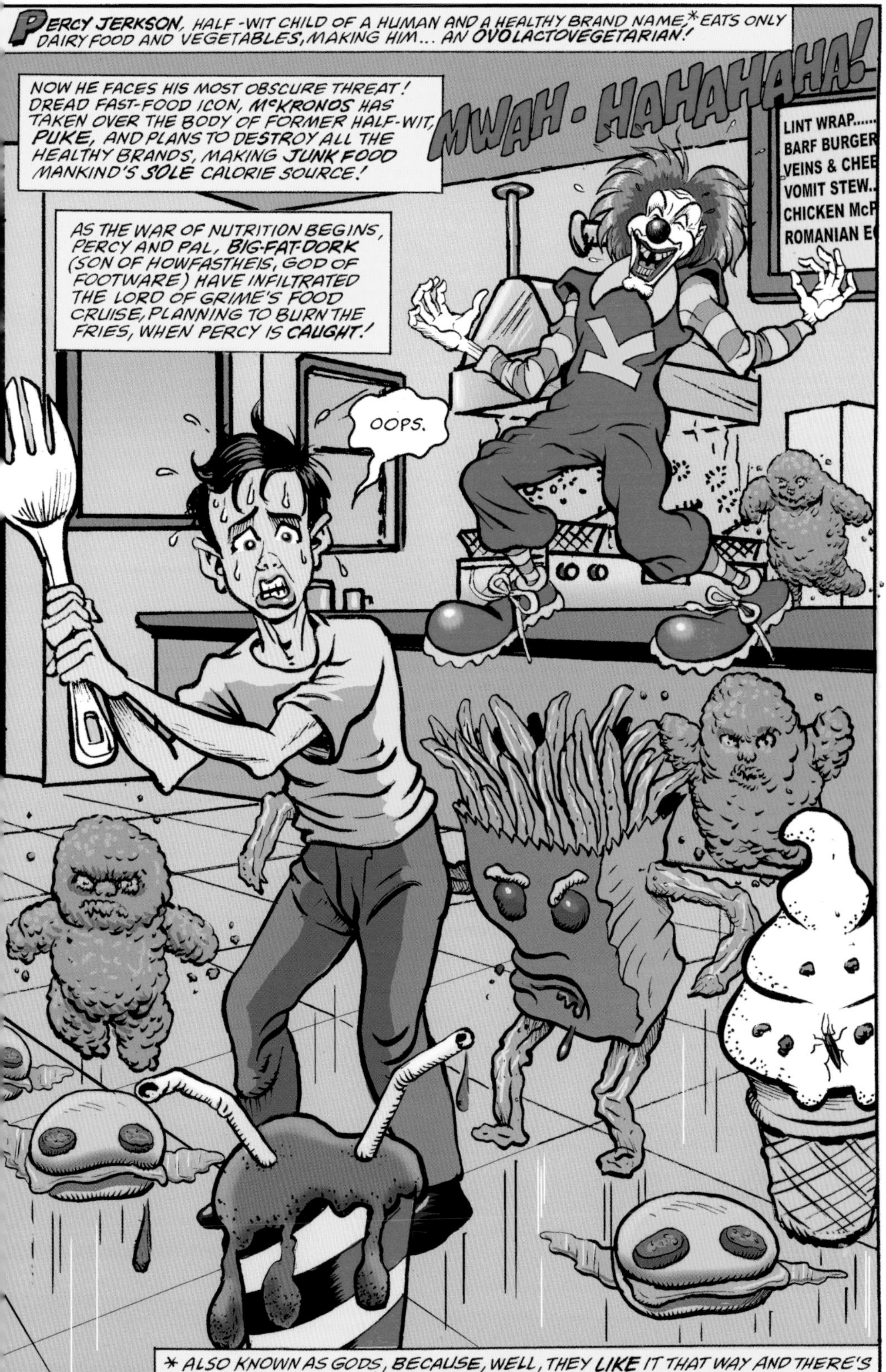
PERCY JERKSON, HALF-WIT CHILD OF A HUMAN AND A HEALTHY BRAND NAME,* EATS ONLY DAIRY FOOD AND VEGETABLES, MAKING HIM... AN OVOLACTOVEGETARIAN!
NOW HE FACES HIS MOST OBSCURE THREAT! DREAD FAST-FOOD ICON, McKRONOS HAS TAKEN OVER THE BODY OF FORMER HALF-WIT, PUKE, AND PLANS TO DESTROY ALL THE HEALTHY BRANDS, MAKING JUNK FOOD MANKIND'S SOLE CALORIE SOURCE!
MWAH-HAHAHAHA!
LINT WRAP......
BARF BURGER
VEINS & CHEE
VOMIT STEW..
CHICKEN McP
ROMANIAN E
AS THE WAR OF NUTRITION BEGINS, PERCY AND PAL, BIG-FAT-DORK (SON OF HOWFASTHEIS, GOD OF FOOTWARE) HAVE INFILTRATED THE LORD OF GRIME'S FOOD CRUISE, PLANNING TO BURN THE FRIES, WHEN PERCY IS CAUGHT!
OOPS.
* ALSO KNOWN AS GODS, BECAUSE, WELL, THEY LIKE IT THAT WAY AND THERE'S JUST NO ARGUING WITH THEM.

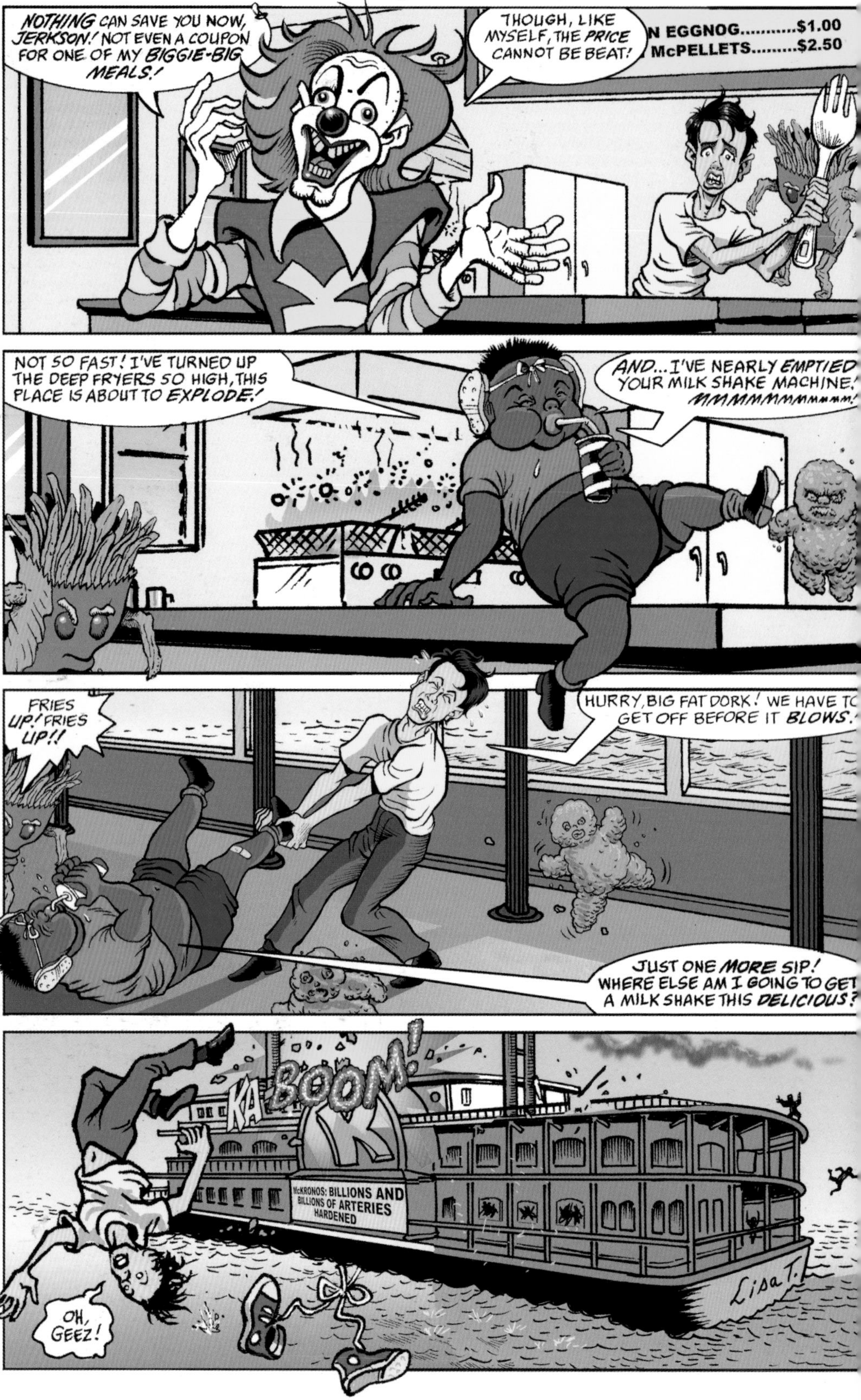
NOTHING CAN SAVE YOU NOW, JERKSON! NOT EVEN A COUPON FOR ONE OF MY BIGGIE-BIG MEALS!
THOUGH, LIKE MYSELF, THE PRICE CANNOT BE BEAT!
N EGGNOG...........$1.00
McPELLETS.........$2.50
NOT SO FAST! I'VE TURNED UP THE DEEP FRYERS SO HIGH, THIS PLACE IS ABOUT TO EXPLODE!
AND...I'VE NEARLY EMPTIED YOUR MILK SHAKE MACHINE! MMMMMMMmmmm!
FRIES UP! FRIES UP!!
HURRY, BIG FAT DORK! WE HAVE TO GET OFF BEFORE IT BLOWS!
JUST ONE MORE SIP! WHERE ELSE AM I GOING TO GET A MILK SHAKE THIS DELICIOUS?
KA BOOM!
McKRONOS: BILLIONS AND BILLIONS OF ARTERIES HARDENED
OH, GEEZ!
Lisa T.

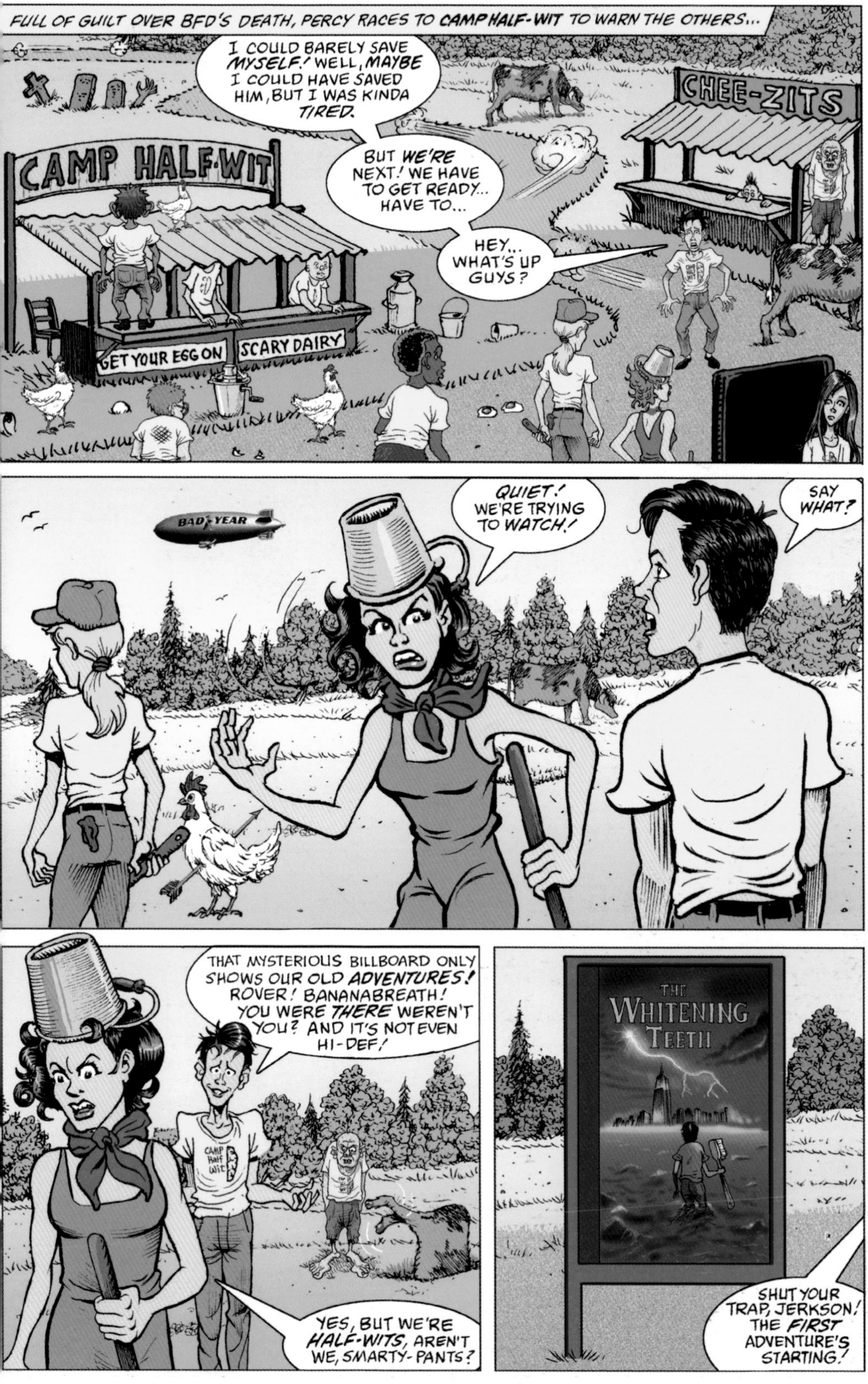
FULL OF GUILT OVER BFD'S DEATH, PERCY RACES TO CAMP HALF-WIT TO WARN THE OTHERS...
CHEE-ZITS
CAMP HALF-WIT
I COULD BARELY SAVE MYSELF! WELL, MAYBE I COULD HAVE SAVED HIM, BUT I WAS KINDA TIRED.
BUT WE'RE NEXT! WE HAVE TO GET READY... HAVE TO...
HEY... WHAT'S UP GUYS?
GET YOUR EGG ON
SCARY DAIRY
BAD YEAR
QUIET! WE'RE TRYING TO WATCH!
SAY WHAT?
THAT MYSTERIOUS BILLBOARD ONLY SHOWS OUR OLD ADVENTURES! ROVER! BANANABREATH! YOU WERE THERE WEREN'T YOU? AND IT'S NOT EVEN HI-DEF!
YES, BUT WE'RE HALF-WITS, AREN'T WE, SMARTY-PANTS?
THE WHITENING TEETH
SHUT YOUR TRAP, JERKSON! THE FIRST ADVENTURE'S STARTING!

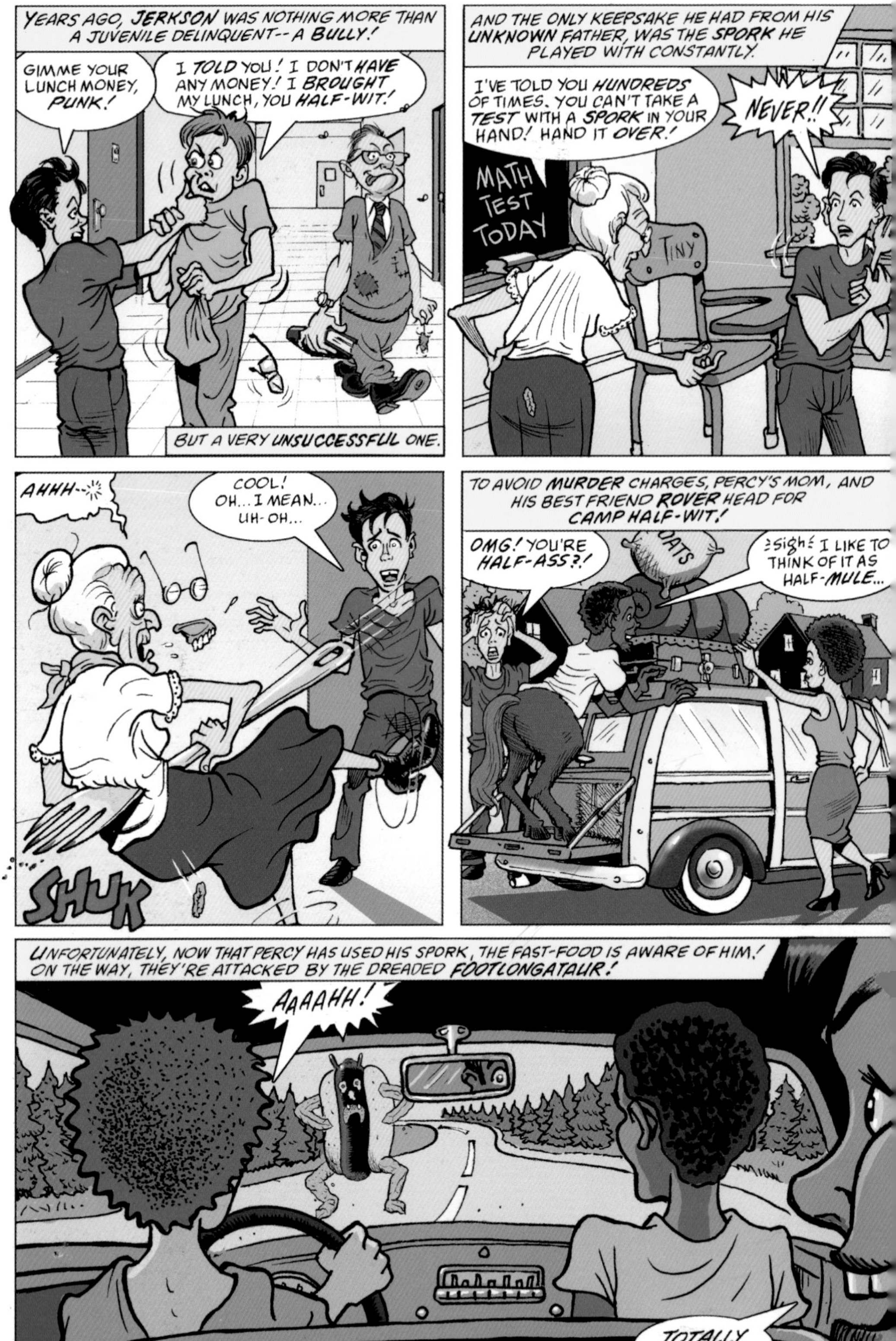
YEARS AGO, JERKSON WAS NOTHING MORE THAN A JUVENILE DELINQUENT-- A BULLY!
GIMME YOUR LUNCH MONEY, PUNK!
I TOLD YOU! I DON'T HAVE ANY MONEY! I BROUGHT MY LUNCH, YOU HALF-WIT!
BUT A VERY UNSUCCESSFUL ONE.
AND THE ONLY KEEPSAKE HE HAD FROM HIS UNKNOWN FATHER, WAS THE SPORK HE PLAYED WITH CONSTANTLY.
I'VE TOLD YOU HUNDREDS OF TIMES. YOU CAN'T TAKE A TEST WITH A SPORK IN YOUR HAND! HAND IT OVER!
NEVER!!
MATH TEST TODAY
TINY
AHHH--
COOL! OH... I MEAN... UH-OH...
SHUK
TO AVOID MURDER CHARGES, PERCY'S MOM, AND HIS BEST FRIEND ROVER HEAD FOR CAMP HALF-WIT!
OMG! YOU'RE HALF-ASS?!
OATS
sigh I LIKE TO THINK OF IT AS HALF-MULE...
UNFORTUNATELY, NOW THAT PERCY HAS USED HIS SPORK, THE FAST-FOOD IS AWARE OF HIM! ON THE WAY, THEY'RE ATTACKED BY THE DREADED FOOTLONGATAUR!
AAAAHH!
TOTALLY COOL!

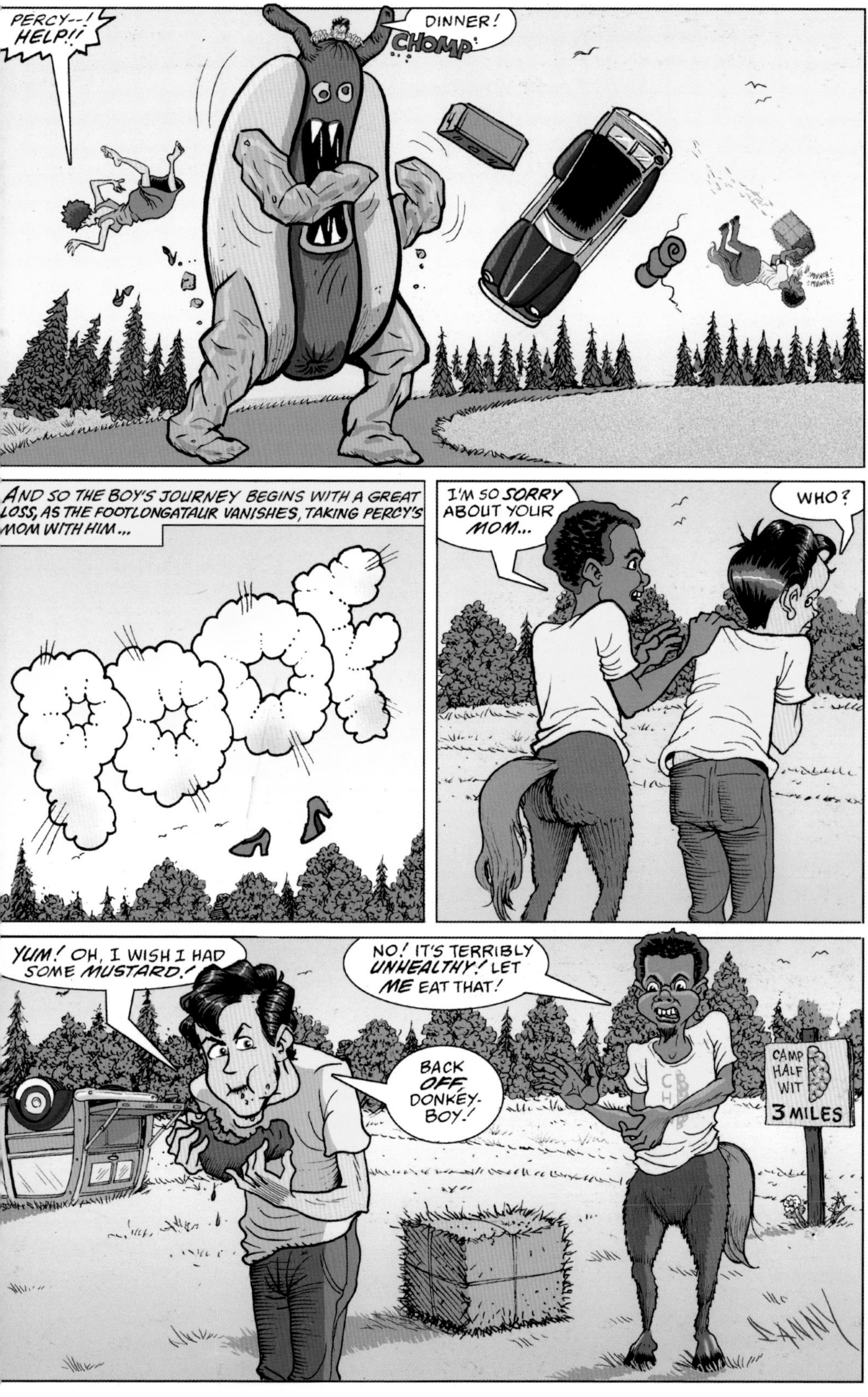
PERCY--! HELP!!
DINNER!
CHOMP
MUNCH MUNCH
AND SO THE BOY'S JOURNEY BEGINS WITH A GREAT LOSS, AS THE FOOTLONGATAUR VANISHES, TAKING PERCY'S MOM WITH HIM...
POOF
I'M SO SORRY ABOUT YOUR MOM...
WHO?
YUM! OH, I WISH I HAD SOME MUSTARD!
NO! IT'S TERRIBLY UNHEALTHY! LET ME EAT THAT!
BACK OFF, DONKEY-BOY!
CAMP HALF WIT
3 MILES
DANNY

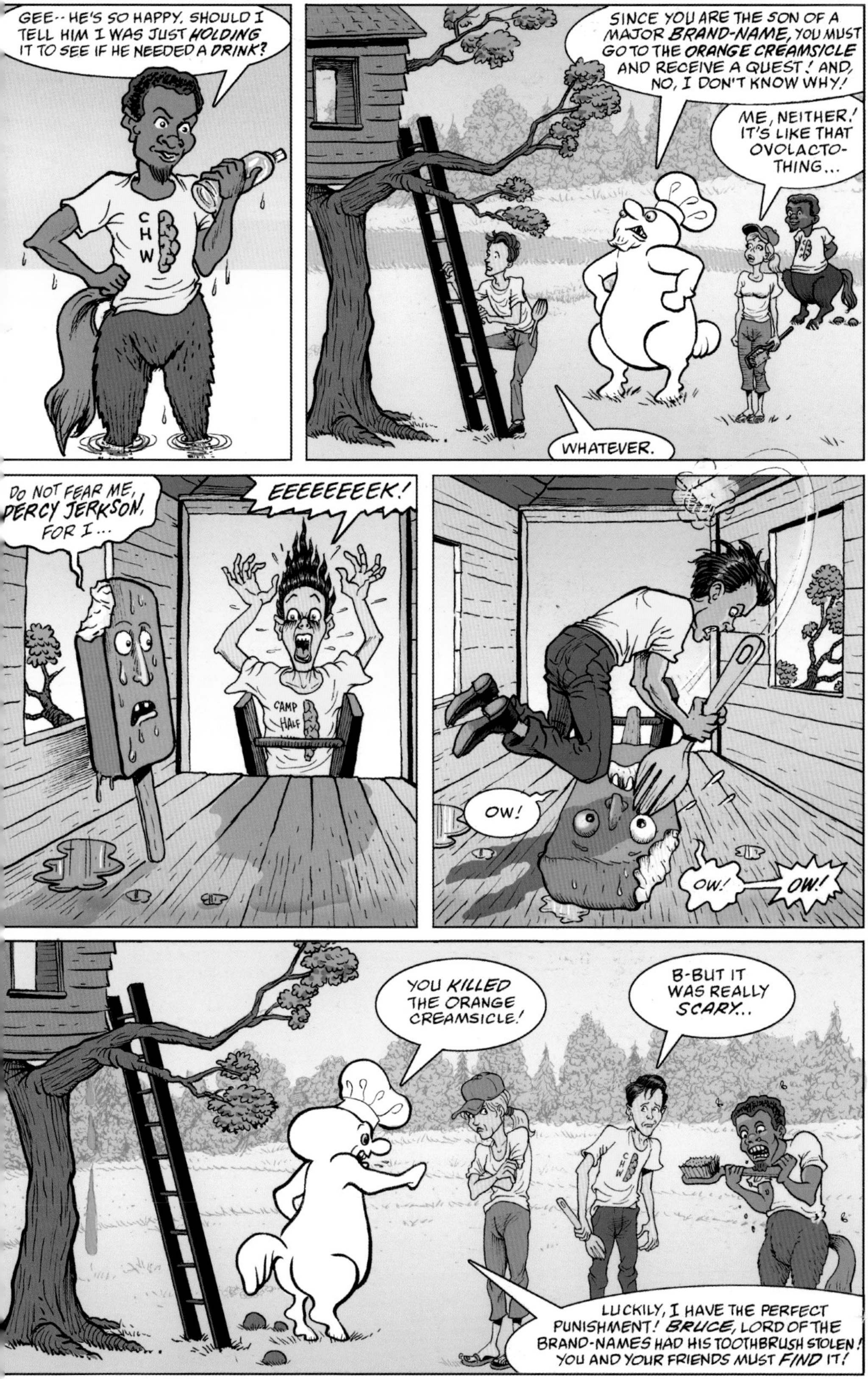
GEE-- HE'S SO HAPPY. SHOULD I TELL HIM I WAS JUST HOLDING IT TO SEE IF HE NEEDED A DRINK?
SINCE YOU ARE THE SON OF A MAJOR BRAND-NAME, YOU MUST GO TO THE ORANGE CREAMSICLE AND RECEIVE A QUEST! AND, NO, I DON'T KNOW WHY!
ME, NEITHER! IT'S LIKE THAT OVOLACTO-THING...
WHATEVER.
CHW
DO NOT FEAR ME, PERCY JERKSON, FOR I...
EEEEEEEEK!
CAMP HALF
OW!
OW!
OW!
YOU KILLED THE ORANGE CREAMSICLE!
B-BUT IT WAS REALLY SCARY...
LUCKILY, I HAVE THE PERFECT PUNISHMENT! BRUCE, LORD OF THE BRAND-NAMES HAD HIS TOOTHBRUSH STOLEN! YOU AND YOUR FRIENDS MUST FIND IT!

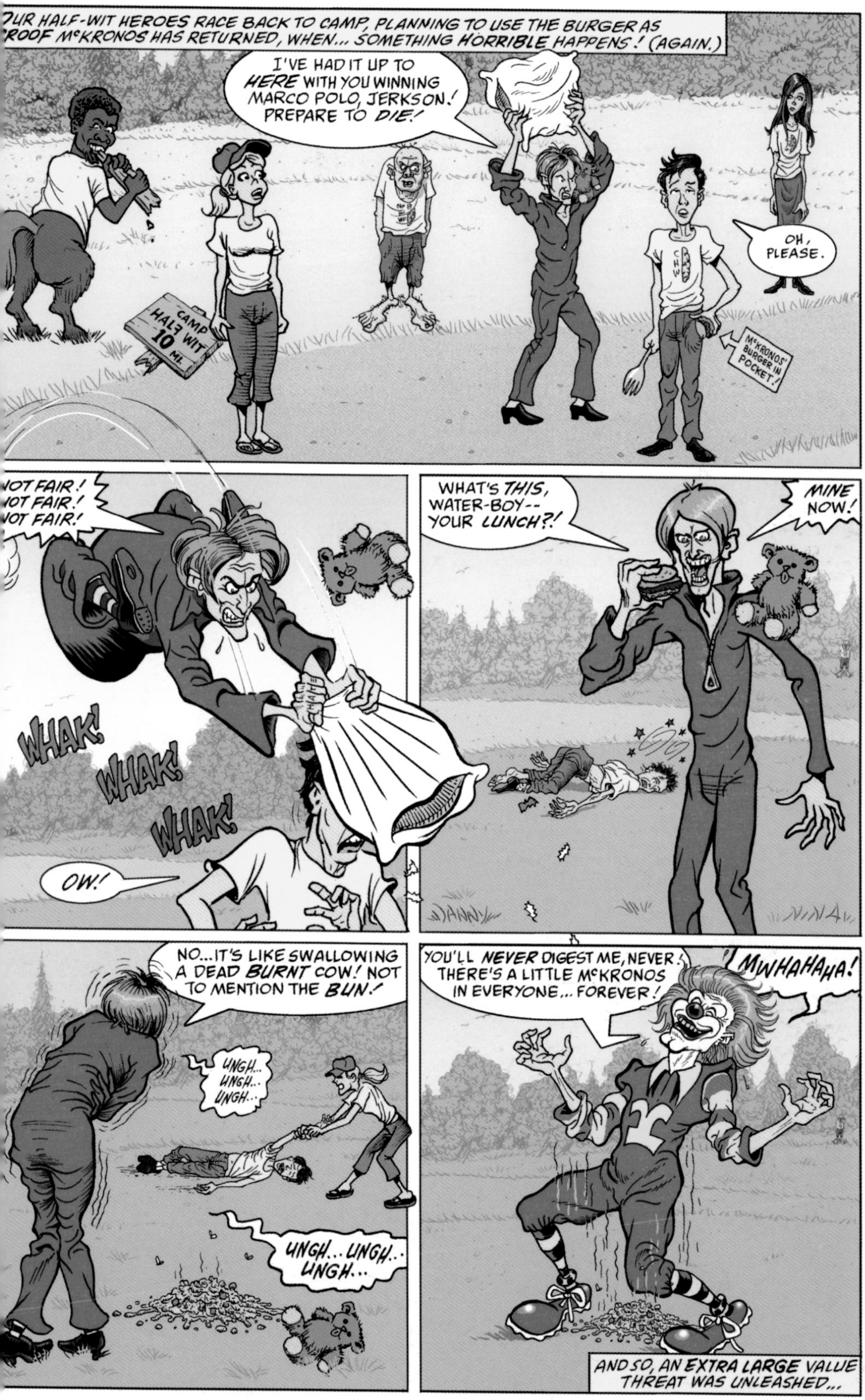
OUR HALF-WIT HEROES RACE BACK TO CAMP, PLANNING TO USE THE BURGER AS PROOF McKRONOS HAS RETURNED, WHEN... SOMETHING HORRIBLE HAPPENS! (AGAIN.)
I'VE HAD IT UP TO HERE WITH YOU WINNING MARCO POLO, JERKSON! PREPARE TO DIE!
OH, PLEASE.
CAMP HALF WIT 10 MI.
McKRONOS' BURGER IN POCKET!
NOT FAIR! NOT FAIR! NOT FAIR!
WHAK! WHAK! WHAK!
OW!
WHAT'S THIS, WATER-BOY-- YOUR LUNCH?!
MINE NOW!
NO...IT'S LIKE SWALLOWING A DEAD BURNT COW! NOT TO MENTION THE BUN!
UNGH... UNGH... UNGH...
UNGH... UNGH... UNGH...
YOU'LL NEVER DIGEST ME, NEVER! THERE'S A LITTLE McKRONOS IN EVERYONE... FOREVER!
MWHAHAHAHA!
AND SO, AN EXTRA LARGE VALUE THREAT WAS UNLEASHED...

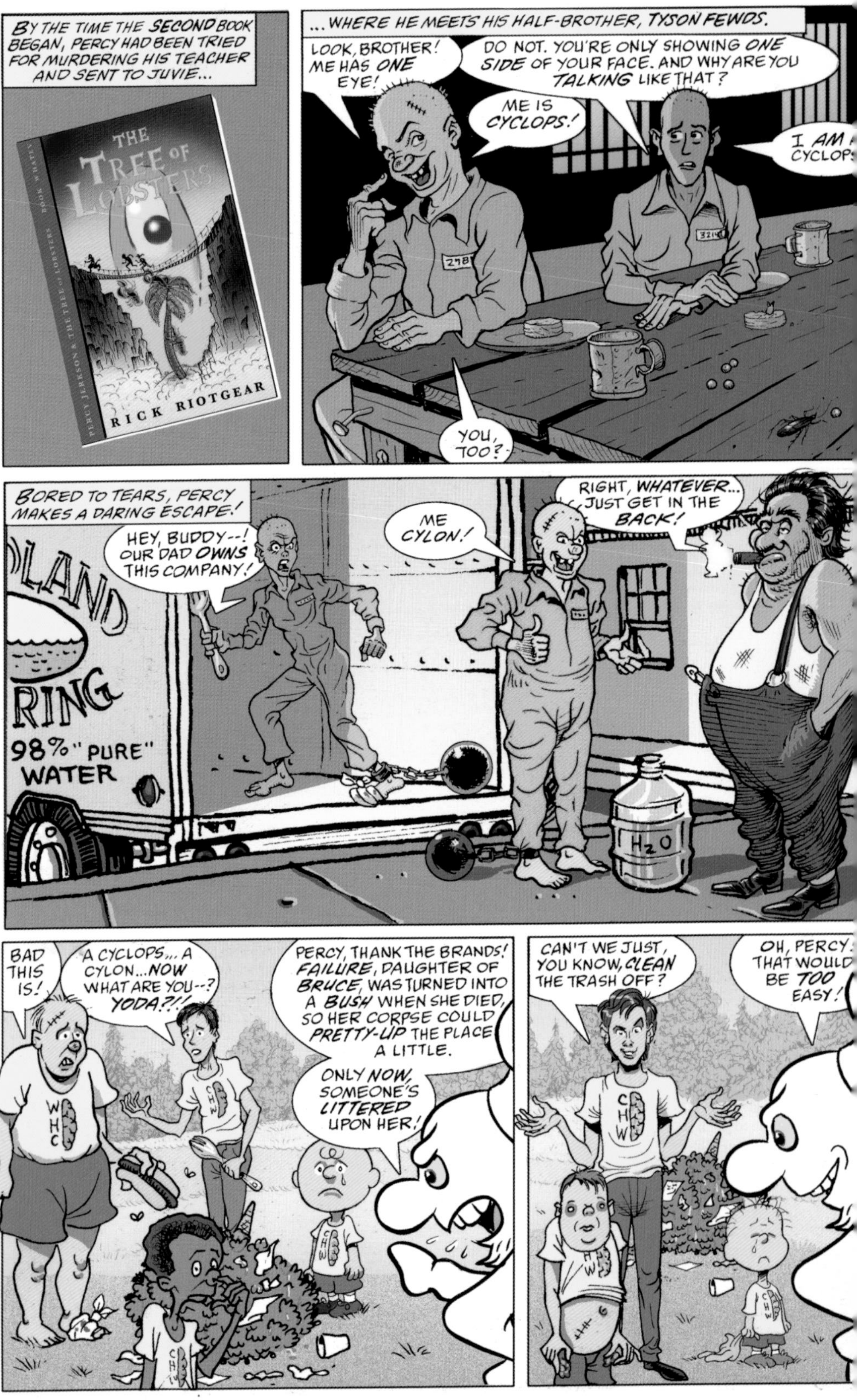

BY THE TIME THE SECOND BOOK BEGAN, PERCY HAD BEEN TRIED FOR MURDERING HIS TEACHER AND SENT TO JUVIE...
THE TREE OF LOBSTERS
PERCY JERKSON & THE TREE OF LOBSTERS BOOK WHATEV
RICK RIOTGEAR
...WHERE HE MEETS HIS HALF-BROTHER, TYSON FEWDS.
LOOK, BROTHER! ME HAS ONE EYE!
DO NOT. YOU'RE ONLY SHOWING ONE SIDE OF YOUR FACE. AND WHY ARE YOU TALKING LIKE THAT?
ME IS CYCLOPS!
I AM
CYCLOPS
YOU, TOO?
BORED TO TEARS, PERCY MAKES A DARING ESCAPE!
HEY, BUDDY--! OUR DAD OWNS THIS COMPANY!
ME CYLON!
RIGHT, WHATEVER... JUST GET IN THE BACK!
OLAND
RING
98% "PURE" WATER
H2O
BAD THIS IS!
A CYCLOPS... A CYLON... NOW WHAT ARE YOU--? YODA?!!
PERCY, THANK THE BRANDS! FAILURE, DAUGHTER OF BRUCE, WAS TURNED INTO A BUSH WHEN SHE DIED, SO HER CORPSE COULD PRETTY-UP THE PLACE A LITTLE.
ONLY NOW, SOMEONE'S LITTERED UPON HER!
CAN'T WE JUST, YOU KNOW, CLEAN THE TRASH OFF?
OH, PERCY!
THAT WOULD BE TOO EASY!

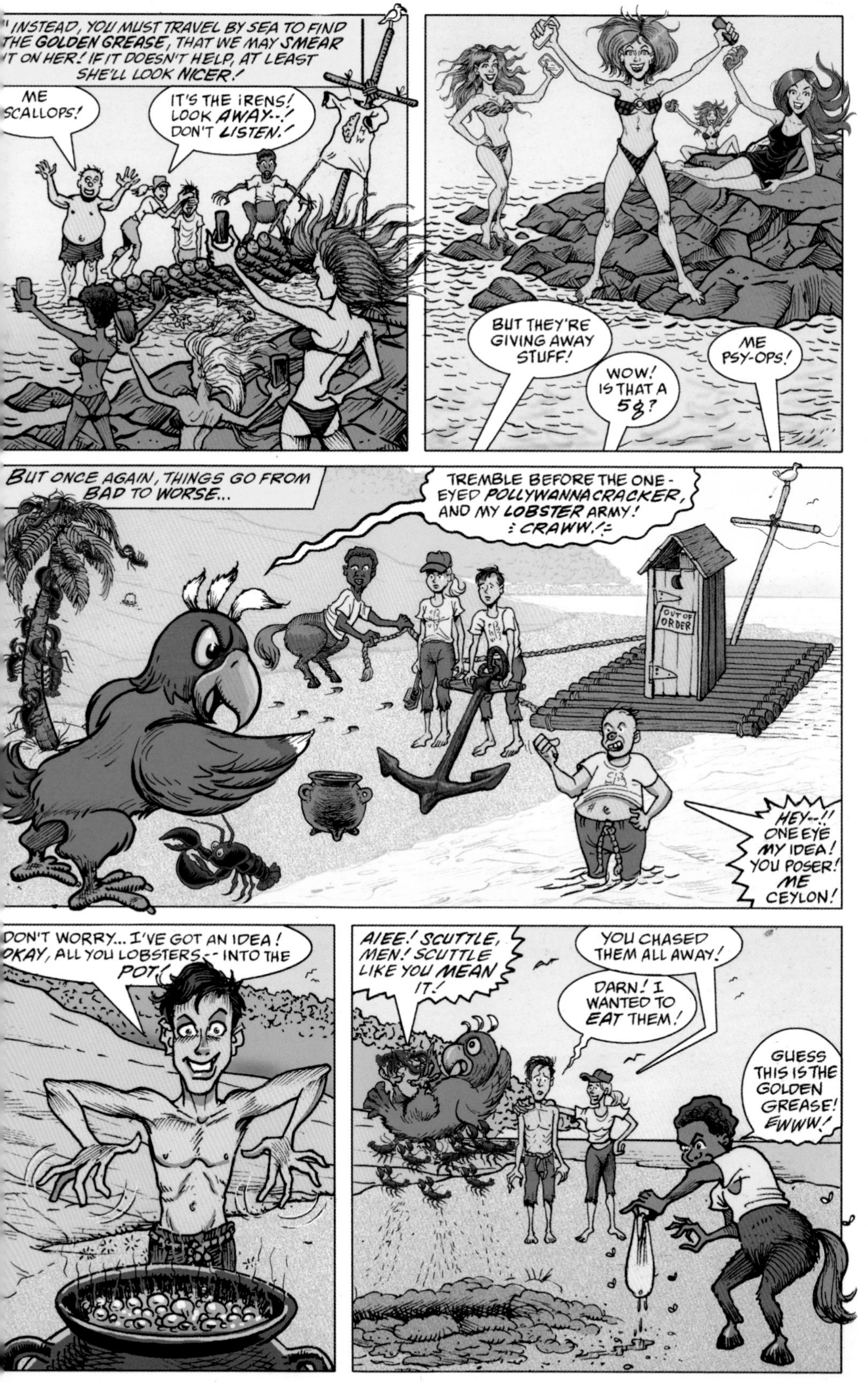

" INSTEAD, YOU MUST TRAVEL BY SEA TO FIND THE GOLDEN GREASE, THAT WE MAY SMEAR T ON HER! IF IT DOESN'T HELP, AT LEAST SHE'LL LOOK NICER!
ME SCALLOPS!
IT'S THE iRENS! LOOK AWAY--! DON'T LISTEN!
BUT THEY'RE GIVING AWAY STUFF!
WOW! IS THAT A 5G?
ME PSY-OPS!
BUT ONCE AGAIN, THINGS GO FROM BAD TO WORSE...
TREMBLE BEFORE THE ONE-EYED POLLYWANNACRACKER, AND MY LOBSTER ARMY! CRAWW!
OUT OF ORDER
HEY--!! ONE EYE MY IDEA! YOU POSER! ME CEYLON!
DON'T WORRY... I'VE GOT AN IDEA! OKAY, ALL YOU LOBSTERS-- INTO THE POT!
AIEE! SCUTTLE, MEN! SCUTTLE LIKE YOU MEAN IT!
YOU CHASED THEM ALL AWAY!
DARN! I WANTED TO EAT THEM!
GUESS THIS IS THE GOLDEN GREASE! EWWW!

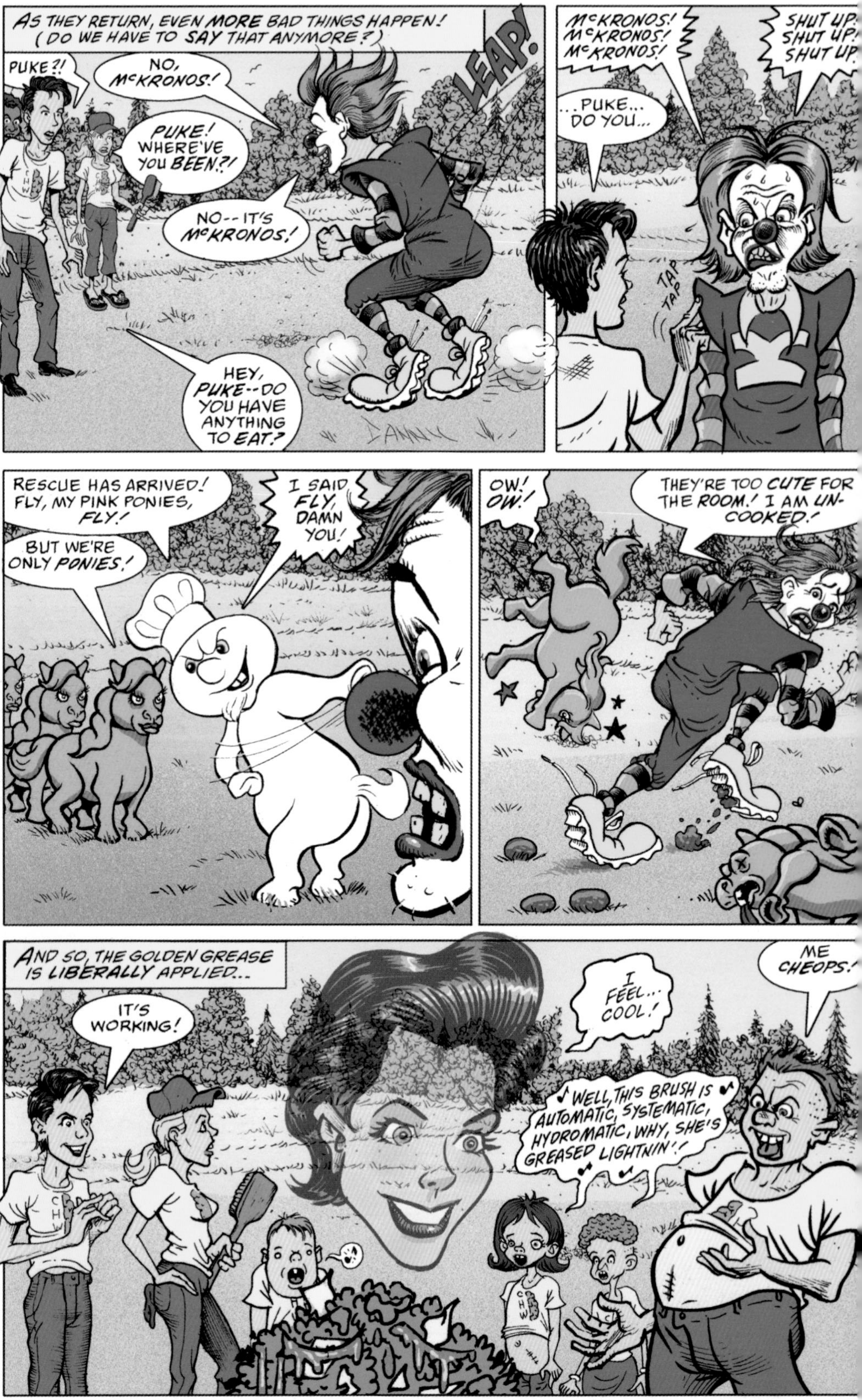
AS THEY RETURN, EVEN MORE BAD THINGS HAPPEN! (DO WE HAVE TO SAY THAT ANYMORE?)
LEAP!
PUKE?!
NO, McKRONOS!
PUKE! WHERE'VE YOU BEEN?!
NO-- IT'S McKRONOS!
HEY, PUKE--DO YOU HAVE ANYTHING TO EAT?
McKRONOS! McKRONOS! McKRONOS!
SHUT UP! SHUT UP! SHUT UP!
...PUKE... DO YOU...
TAP TAP
RESCUE HAS ARRIVED! FLY, MY PINK PONIES, FLY!
I SAID FLY, DAMN YOU!
BUT WE'RE ONLY PONIES!
OW! OW!
THEY'RE TOO CUTE FOR THE ROOM! I AM UN-COOKED!
AND SO, THE GOLDEN GREASE IS LIBERALLY APPLIED...
IT'S WORKING!
I FEEL... COOL!
ME CHEOPS!
WELL, THIS BRUSH IS AUTOMATIC, SYSTEMATIC, HYDROMATIC, WHY, SHE'S GREASED LIGHTNIN'!

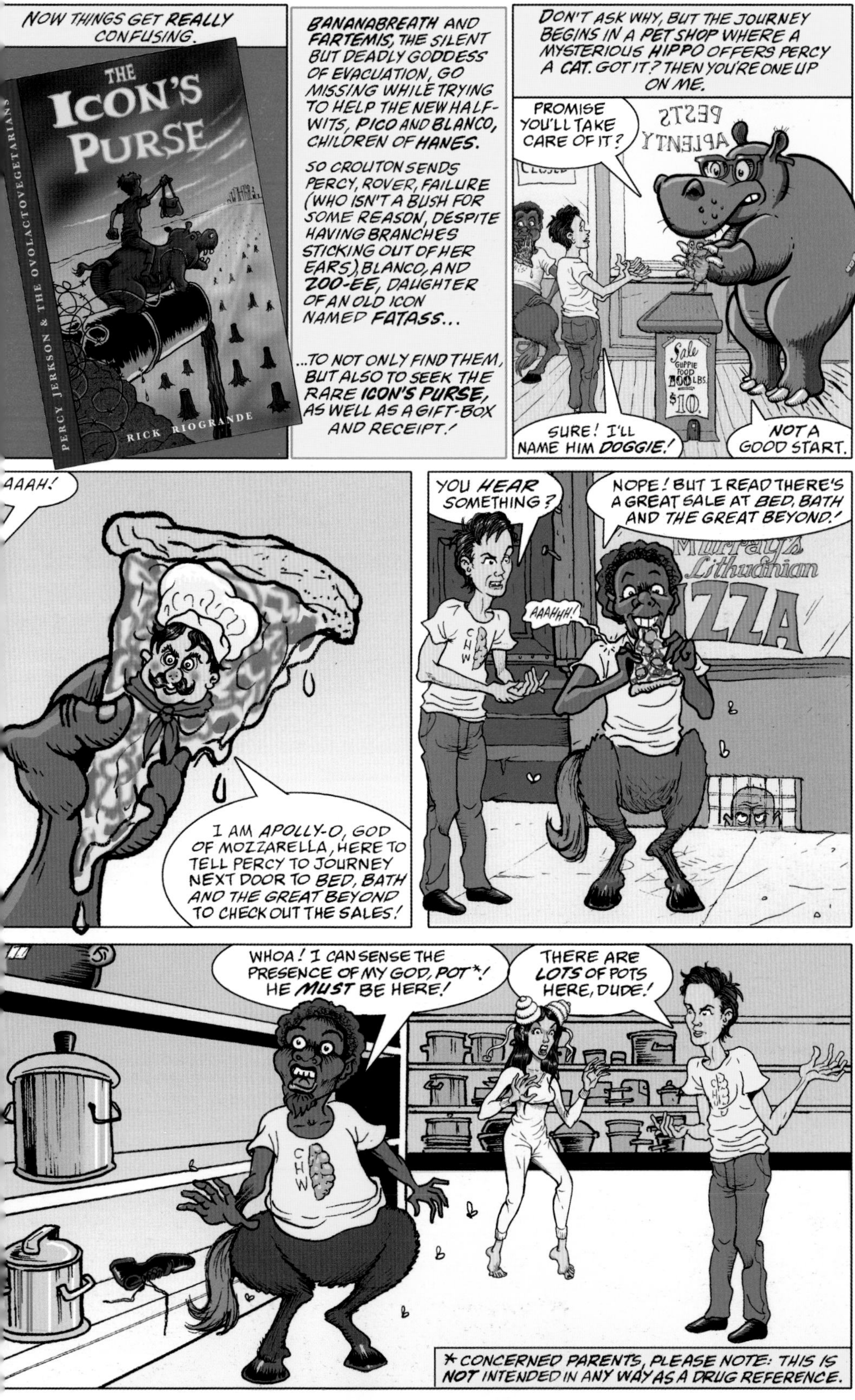
NOW THINGS GET REALLY CONFUSING.
THE ICON'S PURSE
PERCY JERKSON & THE OVOLACTOVEGETARIANS
RICK RIOGRANDE
BANANABREATH AND FARTEMIS, THE SILENT BUT DEADLY GODDESS OF EVACUATION, GO MISSING WHILE TRYING TO HELP THE NEW HALF-WITS, PICO AND BLANCO, CHILDREN OF HANES.
SO CROUTON SENDS PERCY, ROVER, FAILURE (WHO ISN'T A BUSH FOR SOME REASON, DESPITE HAVING BRANCHES STICKING OUT OF HER EARS), BLANCO, AND ZOO-EE, DAUGHTER OF AN OLD ICON NAMED FATASS...
...TO NOT ONLY FIND THEM, BUT ALSO TO SEEK THE RARE ICON'S PURSE, AS WELL AS A GIFT-BOX AND RECEIPT!
DON'T ASK WHY, BUT THE JOURNEY BEGINS IN A PET SHOP WHERE A MYSTERIOUS HIPPO OFFERS PERCY A CAT. GOT IT? THEN YOU'RE ONE UP ON ME.
PESTS APLENTY
PROMISE YOU'LL TAKE CARE OF IT?
Sale GUPPIE FOOD 100 LBS. $10.
SURE! I'LL NAME HIM DOGGIE!
NOT A GOOD START.
AAAH!
I AM APOLLY-O, GOD OF MOZZARELLA, HERE TO TELL PERCY TO JOURNEY NEXT DOOR TO BED, BATH AND THE GREAT BEYOND TO CHECK OUT THE SALES!
YOU HEAR SOMETHING?
NOPE! BUT I READ THERE'S A GREAT SALE AT BED, BATH AND THE GREAT BEYOND!
Murray's Lithuanian IZZA
AAAHHH!
WHOA! I CAN SENSE THE PRESENCE OF MY GOD, POT*! HE MUST BE HERE!
THERE ARE LOTS OF POTS HERE, DUDE!
*CONCERNED PARENTS, PLEASE NOTE: THIS IS NOT INTENDED IN ANY WAY AS A DRUG REFERENCE.

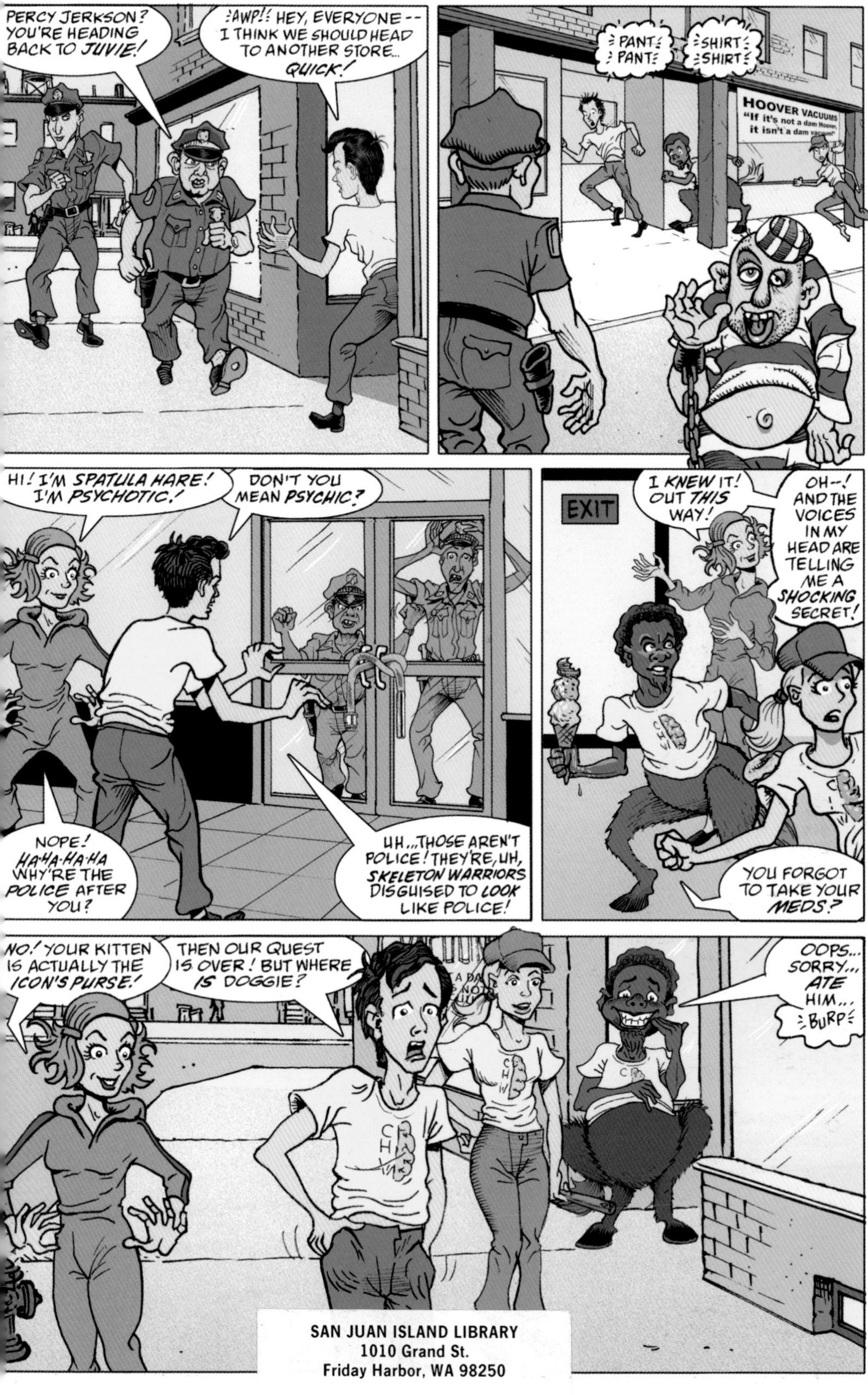
PERCY JERKSON? YOU'RE HEADING BACK TO JUVIE!
AWP!! HEY, EVERYONE -- I THINK WE SHOULD HEAD TO ANOTHER STORE... QUICK!
PANT PANT
SHIRT SHIRT
HOOVER VACUUMS
"If it's not a dam Hoover, it isn't a dam vacuum!"
HI! I'M SPATULA HARE! I'M PSYCHOTIC!
DON'T YOU MEAN PSYCHIC?
NOPE! HA-HA-HA-HA WHY'RE THE POLICE AFTER YOU?
UH... THOSE AREN'T POLICE! THEY'RE, UH, SKELETON WARRIORS DISGUISED TO LOOK LIKE POLICE!
EXIT
I KNEW IT! OUT THIS WAY!
OH--! AND THE VOICES IN MY HEAD ARE TELLING ME A SHOCKING SECRET!
YOU FORGOT TO TAKE YOUR MEDS?
NO! YOUR KITTEN IS ACTUALLY THE ICON'S PURSE!
THEN OUR QUEST IS OVER! BUT WHERE IS DOGGIE?
OOPS... SORRY... ATE HIM... BURP

OH, WELL. WE STILL HAVE TO FIND *BANANABREATH* AND *FARTEMIS!* AND THAT MEANS...*ROAD TRIP!*

BUT FIRST, A QUICK STOP AT...*THE OLIVE GARDEN!*

COME TO THINK OF IT, *NONE* OF US EAT LIKE OVOLACTOVEGETERIANS!

YEAH, BUT *THIS* IS TOTALLY AMAZING!

WHOEVER HEARD OF AN *ITALIAN* RESTAURANT SERVING FORTUNE COOKIES?

GO 2 DA ICON CAPITTAL IN OLD GYM CUZ DAT'S WERE YOU WILL FIND YER FRI...

MEANWHILE, AT THE ICON CAPITAL ALL KINDS OF STUFF IS HAPPENING...

FATASS, YOU MONSTER! YOU TRICKED ME INTO HOLDING UP THIS OVERWEIGHT MAN WHEN *YOU'RE* THE ONE WHO NEEDS THE EXERCISE!

MEN'S ROOM

KEEP OUT

HA! THAT GOT HIT IN THE HEAD WITH *TWO* COCONUTS!

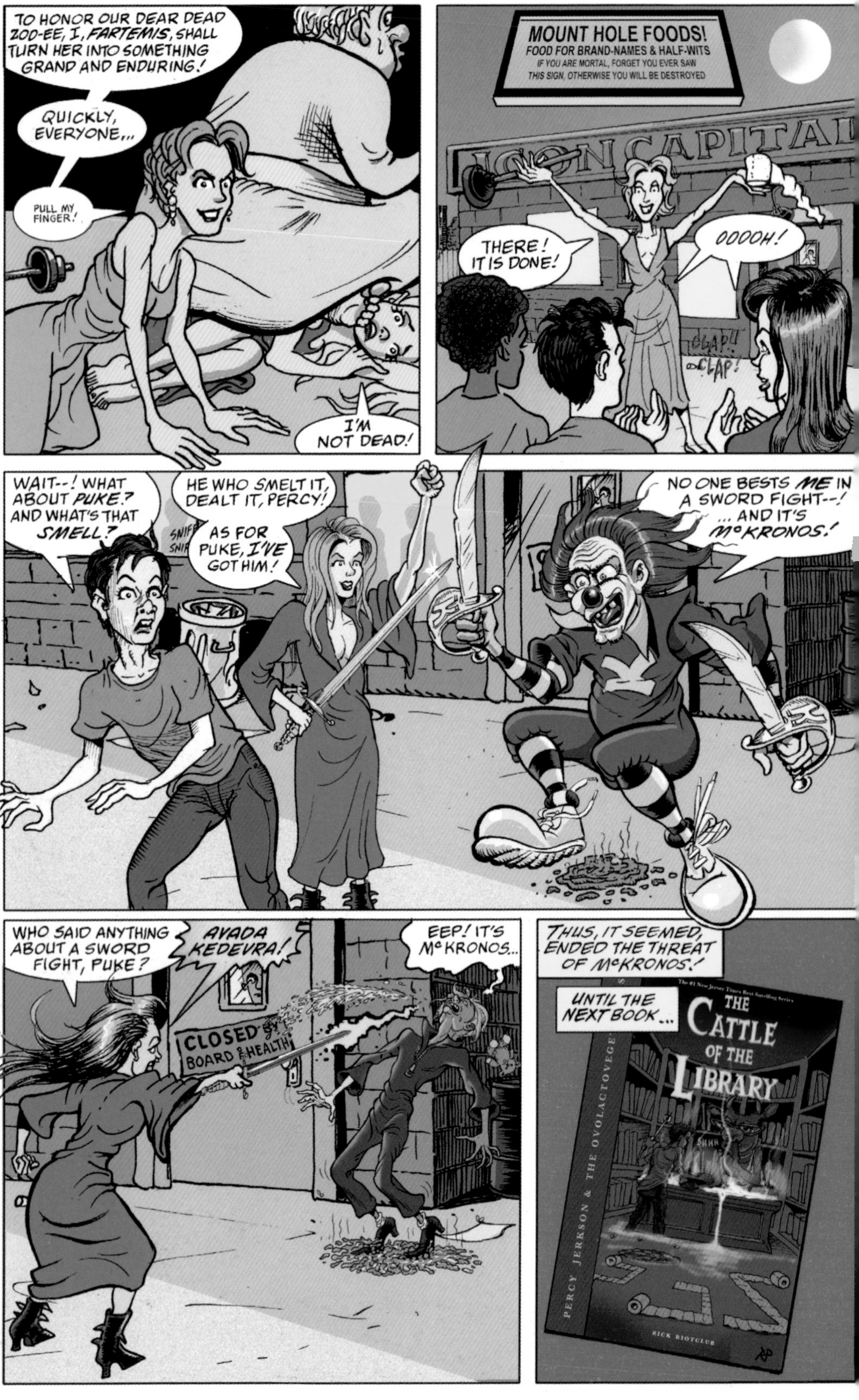
TO HONOR OUR DEAR DEAD ZOO-EE, I, FARTEMIS, SHALL TURN HER INTO SOMETHING GRAND AND ENDURING!
QUICKLY, EVERYONE...
PULL MY FINGER!
I'M NOT DEAD!
MOUNT HOLE FOODS!
FOOD FOR BRAND-NAMES & HALF-WITS
IF YOU ARE MORTAL, FORGET YOU EVER SAW THIS SIGN, OTHERWISE YOU WILL BE DESTROYED
ICON CAPITAL
THERE! IT IS DONE!
OOOOH!
CLAP! CLAP!
WAIT--! WHAT ABOUT PUKE? AND WHAT'S THAT SMELL?
HE WHO SMELT IT, DEALT IT, PERCY!
AS FOR PUKE, I'VE GOT HIM!
NO ONE BESTS ME IN A SWORD FIGHT--! ... AND IT'S McKRONOS!
WHO SAID ANYTHING ABOUT A SWORD FIGHT, PUKE?
AVADA KEDEVRA!
EEP! IT'S McKRONOS...
CLOSED BY BOARD OF HEALTH
THUS, IT SEEMED, ENDED THE THREAT OF McKRONOS!
UNTIL THE NEXT BOOK...
The #1 New Jersey Times Best-Smelling Series
THE CATTLE OF THE LIBRARY
PERCY JERKSON & THE OVOLACTOVEGE
SHHH
RICK RIOTCLUB

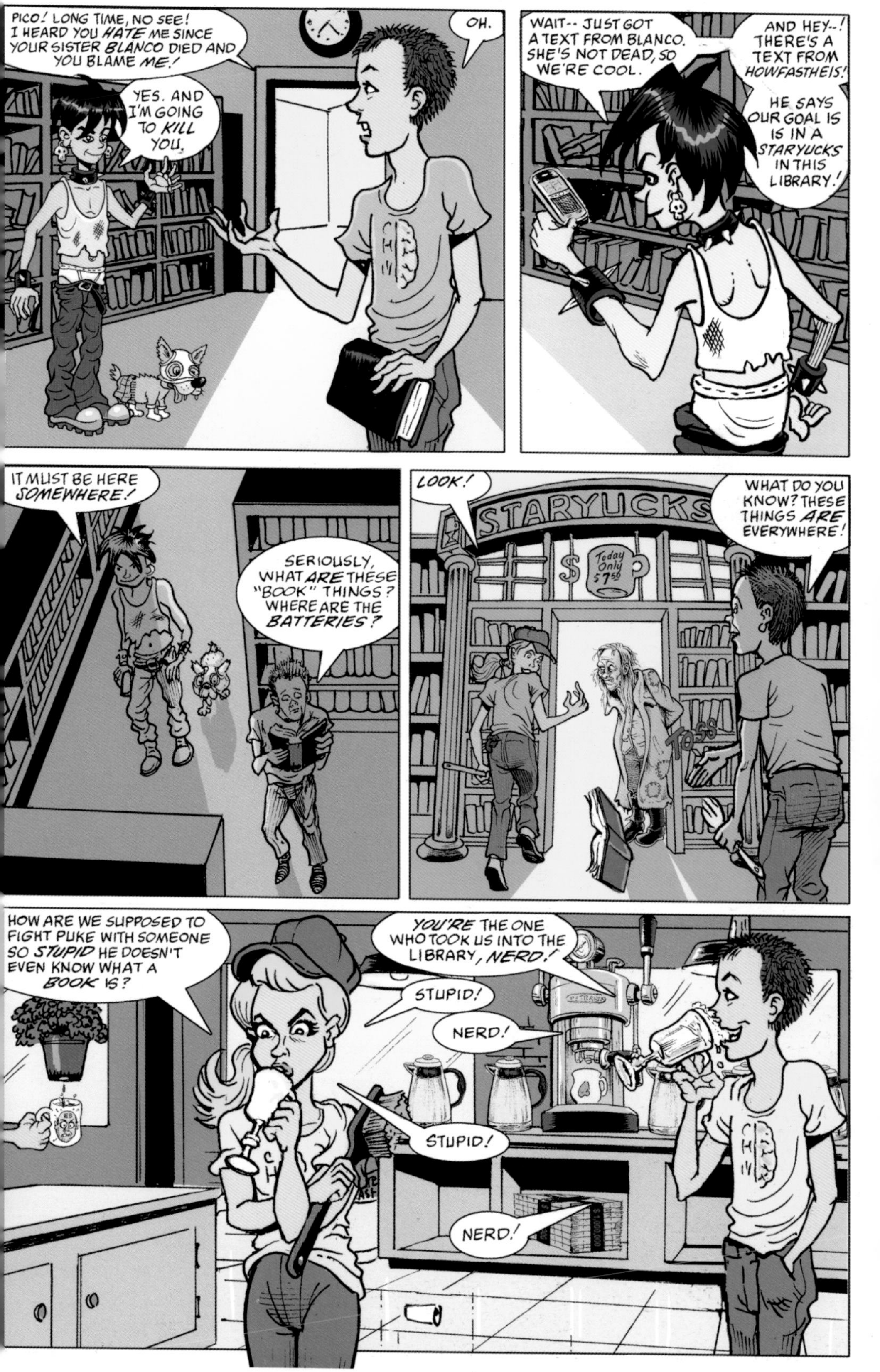
PICO! LONG TIME, NO SEE! I HEARD YOU HATE ME SINCE YOUR SISTER BLANCO DIED AND YOU BLAME ME!
OH.
YES. AND I'M GOING TO KILL YOU.
WAIT-- JUST GOT A TEXT FROM BLANCO. SHE'S NOT DEAD, SO WE'RE COOL.
AND HEY--! THERE'S A TEXT FROM HOWFASTHEIS!
HE SAYS OUR GOAL IS IS IN A STARYUCKS IN THIS LIBRARY!
IT MUST BE HERE SOMEWHERE!
SERIOUSLY, WHAT ARE THESE "BOOK" THINGS? WHERE ARE THE BATTERIES?
LOOK!
STARYUCKS
Today Only $7.50
WHAT DO YOU KNOW? THESE THINGS ARE EVERYWHERE!
TOSS
HOW ARE WE SUPPOSED TO FIGHT PUKE WITH SOMEONE SO STUPID HE DOESN'T EVEN KNOW WHAT A BOOK IS?
YOU'RE THE ONE WHO TOOK US INTO THE LIBRARY, NERD!
STUPID!
NERD!
STUPID!
NERD!

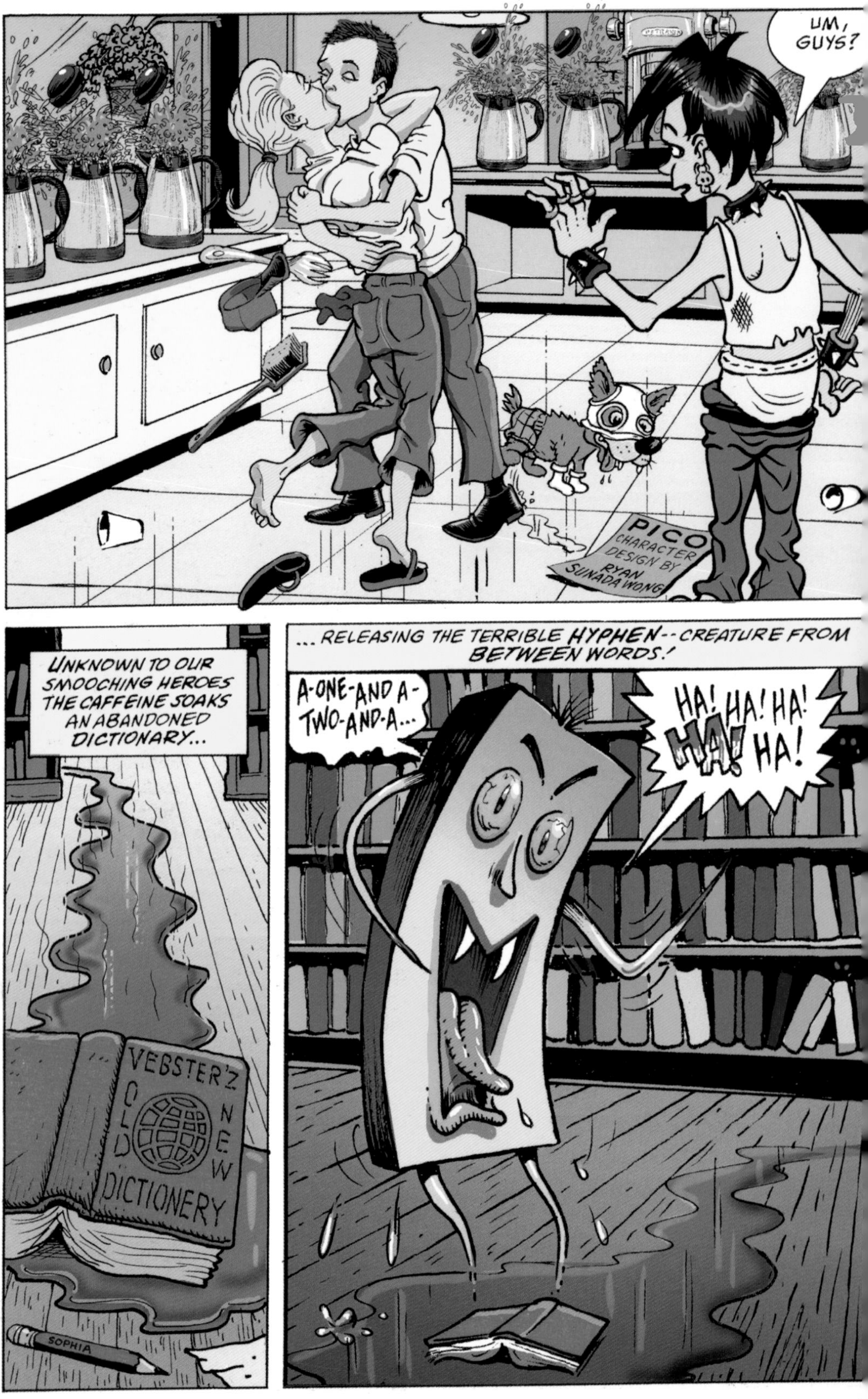
UM, GUYS?
PICO CHARACTER DESIGN BY RYAN SUNADA WONG
UNKNOWN TO OUR SMOOCHING HEROES THE CAFFEINE SOAKS AN ABANDONED DICTIONARY...
VEBSTER'Z OLD NEW DICTIONERY
SOPHIA
... RELEASING THE TERRIBLE HYPHEN--CREATURE FROM BETWEEN WORDS!
A-ONE-AND A-TWO-AND-A...
HA! HA! HA! HA! HA!

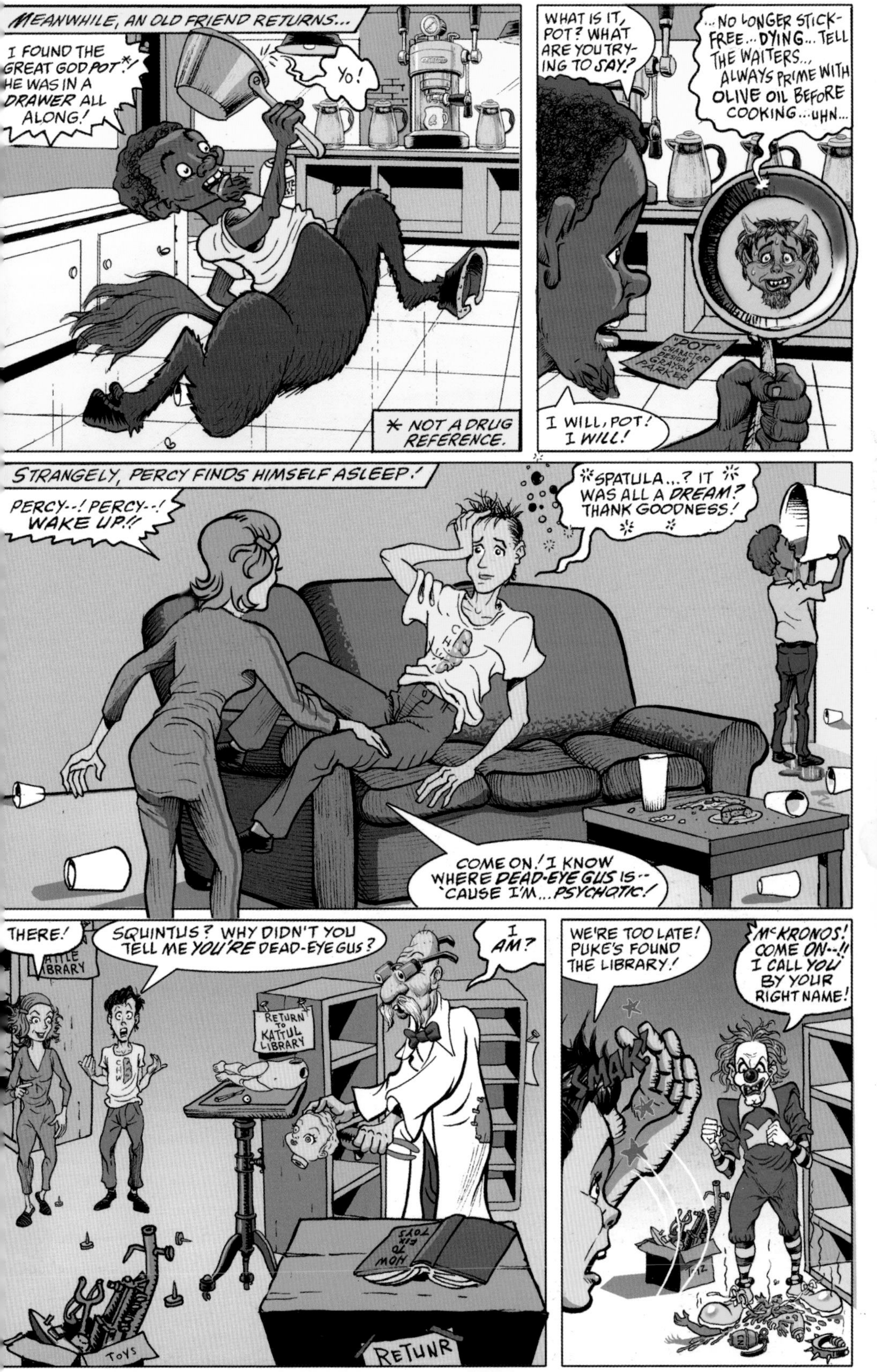
MEANWHILE, AN OLD FRIEND RETURNS...
I FOUND THE GREAT GOD POT*! HE WAS IN A DRAWER ALL ALONG!
YO!
* NOT A DRUG REFERENCE.
WHAT IS IT, POT? WHAT ARE YOU TRYING TO SAY?
...NO LONGER STICK-FREE... DYING... TELL THE WAITERS... ALWAYS PRIME WITH OLIVE OIL BEFORE COOKING...UHN...
"POT" CHARACTER DESIGN BY GRAYSON PARKER
I WILL, POT! I WILL!
STRANGELY, PERCY FINDS HIMSELF ASLEEP!
PERCY--! PERCY--! WAKE UP!!
SPATULA...? IT WAS ALL A DREAM? THANK GOODNESS!
COME ON! I KNOW WHERE DEAD-EYE GUS IS-- 'CAUSE I'M... PSYCHOTIC!
THERE!
SQUINTUS? WHY DIDN'T YOU TELL ME YOU'RE DEAD-EYE GUS?
I AM?
RETURN TO KATTUL LIBRARY
HOW TO FIX TOYS
TOYS
RETUNR
WE'RE TOO LATE! PUKE'S FOUND THE LIBRARY!
McKRONOS! COME ON--!! I CALL YOU BY YOUR RIGHT NAME!
SMAK!

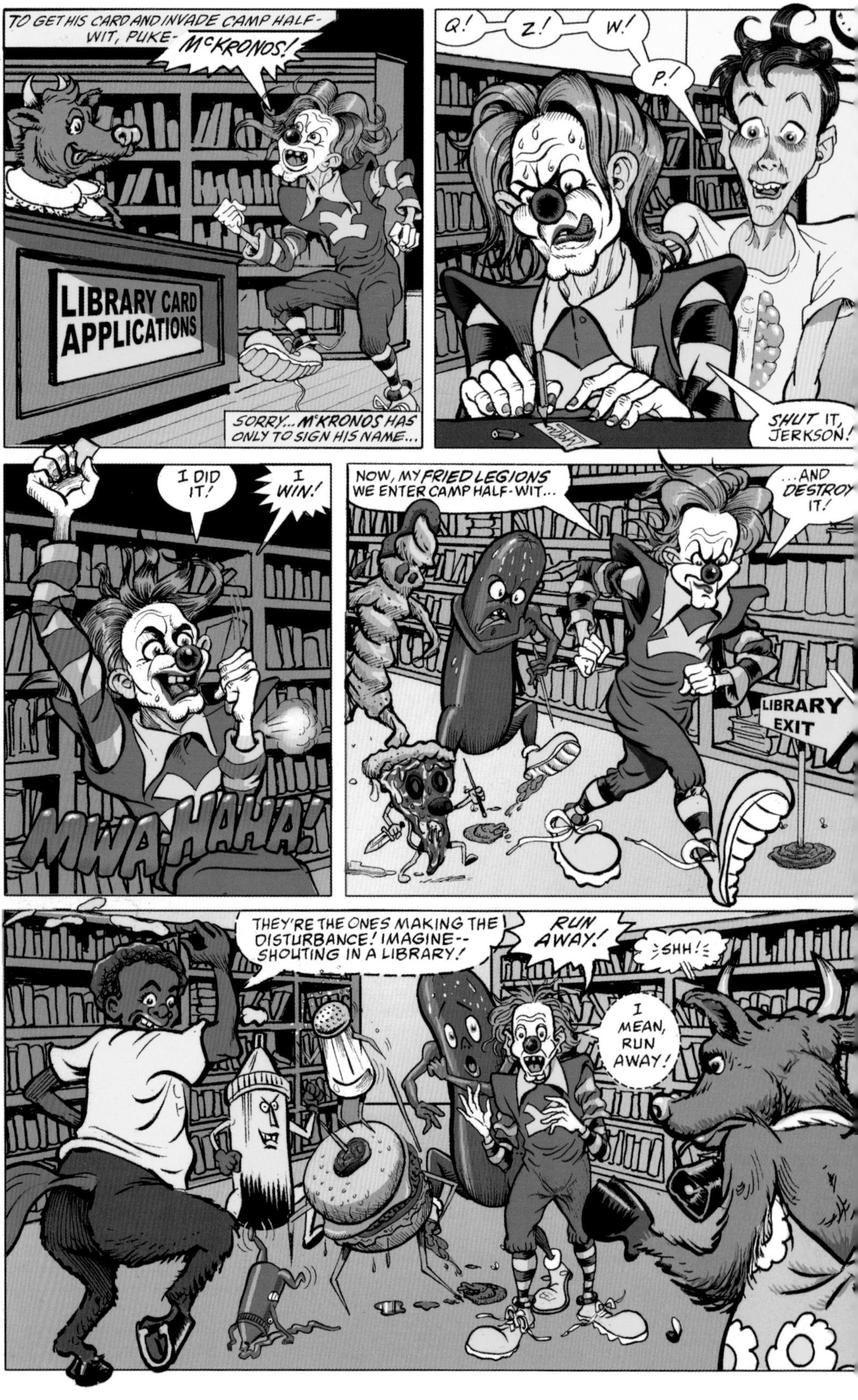
TO GET HIS CARD AND INVADE CAMP HALF-WIT, PUKE-
McKRONOS!
LIBRARY CARD APPLICATIONS
SORRY... McKRONOS HAS ONLY TO SIGN HIS NAME...
Q!
Z!
W!
P!
SHUT IT, JERKSON!
I DID IT!
I WIN!
MWA-HAHA!
NOW, MY FRIED LEGIONS WE ENTER CAMP HALF-WIT...
...AND DESTROY IT!
LIBRARY EXIT
THEY'RE THE ONES MAKING THE DISTURBANCE! IMAGINE-- SHOUTING IN A LIBRARY!
RUN AWAY!
SHH!
I MEAN, RUN AWAY!

OKAY, PEOPLE--MCKRONOS IS GONNA ATTACK, AND... WELL...THAT'LL BE *BAD!* SO, UH... PEOPLE NEED TO *FIGHT* HIM, AND IN ORDER FOR PEOPLE TO FIGHT HIM, WE NEED *PEOPLE!* AND *YOU GUYS* ARE PEOPLE, SORT OF, SO... PEOPLE-- *MOVE OUT!!*

BUT WE *LIKE* IT HERE!

THE CHILDREN OF LARRY WILL *NOT* FIGHT!

AW, *ELBOWGREASE...* WHY DO YOU HAVE TO BE LIKE THAT? COME *ON!* PLEASE *!?*

WHY *SHOULD* WE? YOU GUYS ARE ALWAYS TRACKING *MUD* ON OUR NICE *CLEAN* FLOORS!

HAVE YOU EVER *THANKED* US? SENT SO MUCH AS A *CARD?*

CLOMP

KLOMP

CLOMP

KLOMP

CLOMP

HOW CAN YOU TALK ABOUT *FLOORS* WHEN MY BOYFRIEND BIG FAT DORK IS DEAD?!!

HE DIDN'T BRING BACK SO MUCH AS A *BURGER!* ≈SOB≈

IT'S *TOTALLY* NOT *FAIR.!!*

THERE, THERE! IT'LL BE OKAY, VELVEETA!

PERCY'S *RIGHT!!*

I THINK IT'S A *GOOD* THING HE DIED!

I HEARD HE WAS *CHEATING* ON YOU!

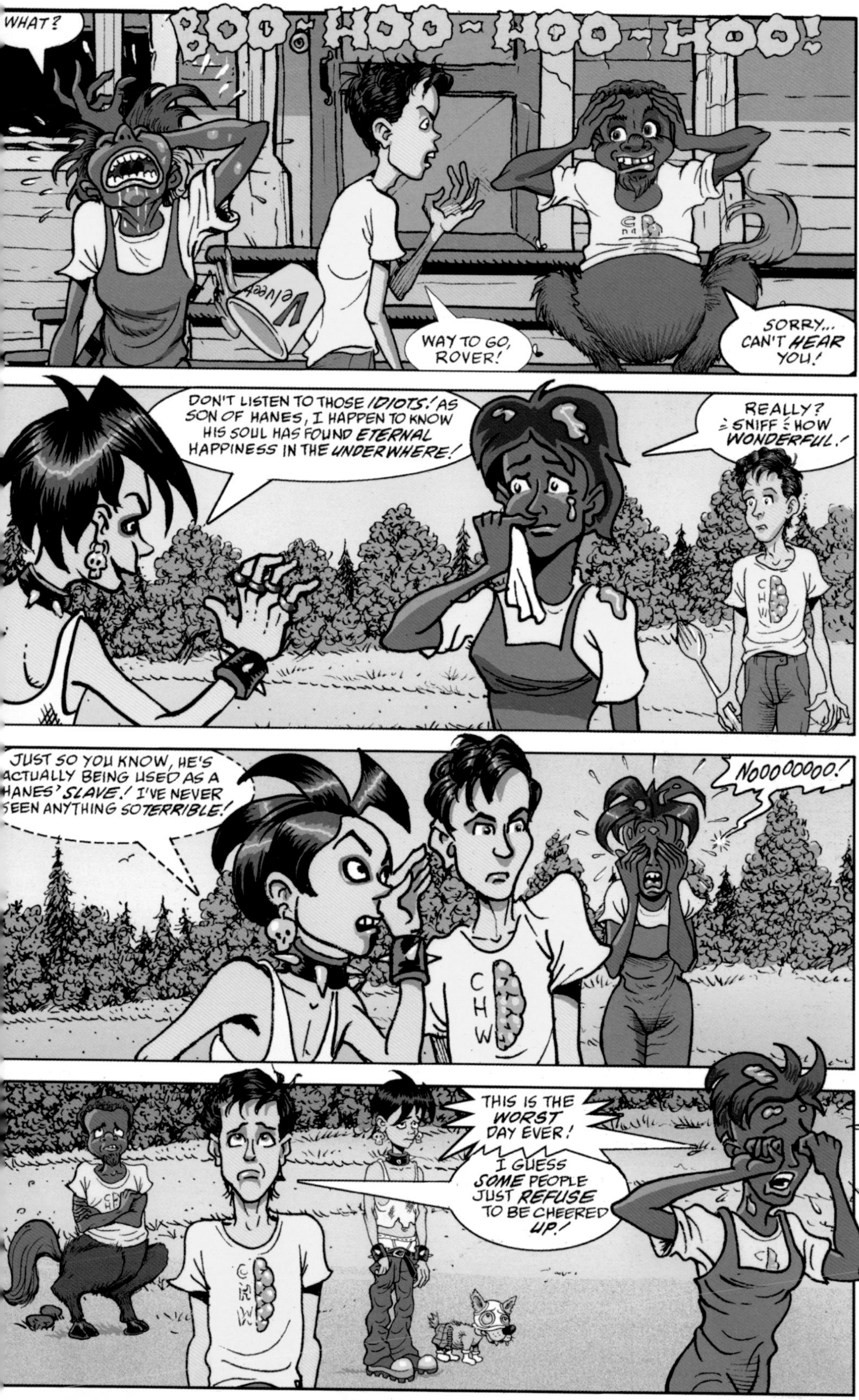
WHAT?
BOO-HOO-HOO-HOO!
WAY TO GO, ROVER!
SORRY... CAN'T HEAR YOU!
DON'T LISTEN TO THOSE IDIOTS! AS SON OF HANES, I HAPPEN TO KNOW HIS SOUL HAS FOUND ETERNAL HAPPINESS IN THE UNDERWHERE!
REALLY? SNIFF HOW WONDERFUL!
JUST SO YOU KNOW, HE'S ACTUALLY BEING USED AS A HANES' SLAVE! I'VE NEVER SEEN ANYTHING SO TERRIBLE!
NOOOOOOO!
THIS IS THE WORST DAY EVER!
I GUESS SOME PEOPLE JUST REFUSE TO BE CHEERED UP!

IF YOU'RE DONE CRUSHING THE MORALE OF YOUR FELLOW CAMPERS, PERCY JERKSON, IT'S TIME YOU LEARNED THE *REALLY GREAT PROPHECY!*

THAT SOUNDS PRETTY GOOD.'

NO--*REALLY GREAT*-- AND IT'S RIGHT UP THERE!

UM ... ON *SECOND* THOUGHT...

THE TIME FOR THOUGHT HAS *PASSED!*

DO YOUR DUTY!

Hee-hee HE SAID *DOODY.*

THE PROPHECY'S WRIT ON THE STICK OF THE CREAMSICLE YOU KILLED.

HAD TO PUT THE BODY SOMEWHERE, EH?

WELL, THAT'S JUST *PERFECT* ISN'T IT?

NO! REALLY *GREAT!* WILL YOU PLEASE *LISTEN?!!*

EC COMICS

EC COMICS

THAT CAN'T BE GOOD.

I KEEP TELLING YOU--

REALLY *GREAT!*

NOW WHAT'S IT SAY?

WE'RE ALL GONNA DIE RUN AWAY RUN AWAY

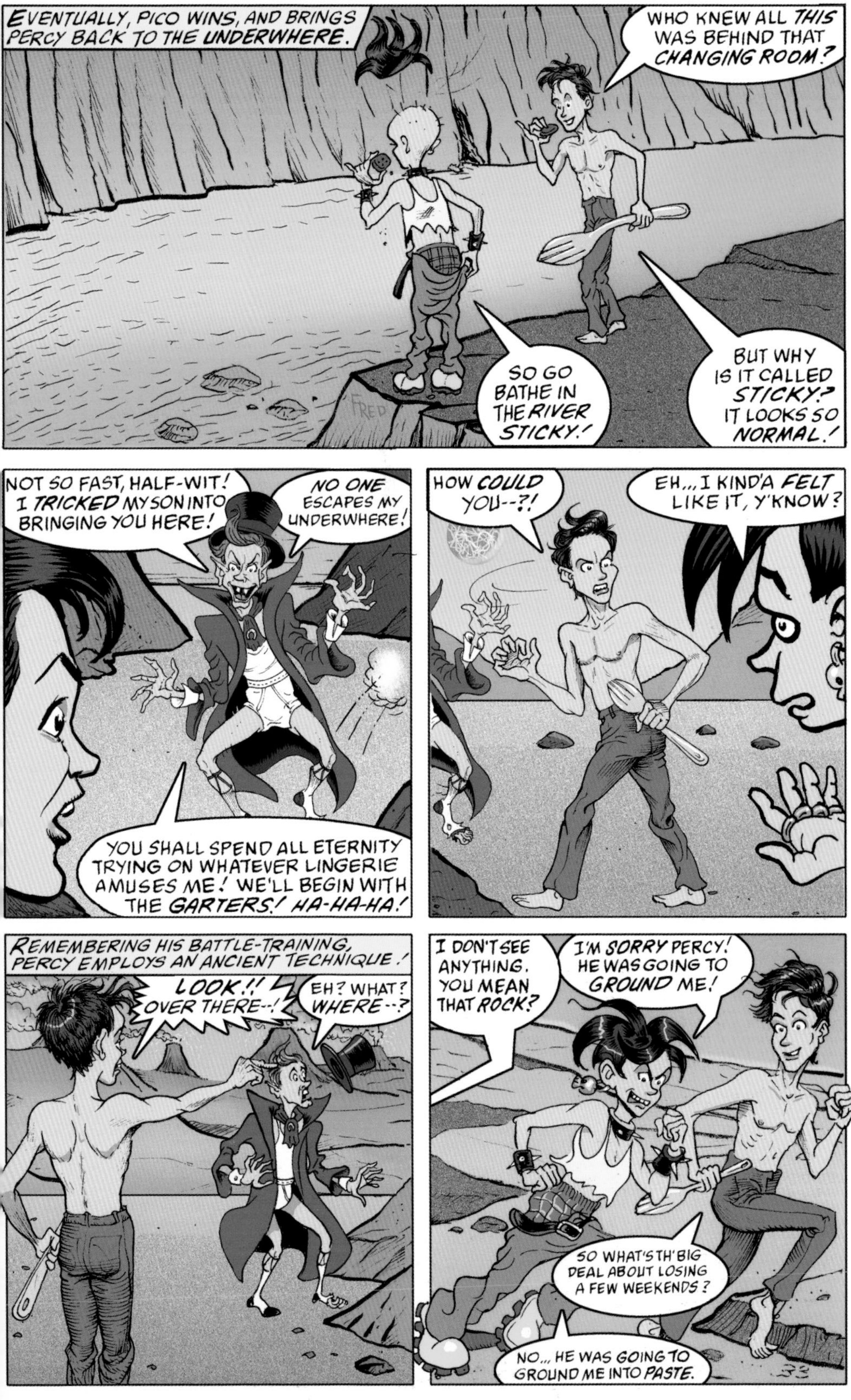
EVENTUALLY, PICO WINS, AND BRINGS PERCY BACK TO THE UNDERWHERE.
WHO KNEW ALL THIS WAS BEHIND THAT CHANGING ROOM?
SO GO BATHE IN THE RIVER STICKY!
BUT WHY IS IT CALLED STICKY? IT LOOKS SO NORMAL!
NOT SO FAST, HALF-WIT! I TRICKED MY SON INTO BRINGING YOU HERE!
NO ONE ESCAPES MY UNDERWHERE!
YOU SHALL SPEND ALL ETERNITY TRYING ON WHATEVER LINGERIE AMUSES ME! WE'LL BEGIN WITH THE GARTERS! HA-HA-HA!
HOW COULD YOU--?!
EH... I KIND'A FELT LIKE IT, Y'KNOW?
REMEMBERING HIS BATTLE-TRAINING, PERCY EMPLOYS AN ANCIENT TECHNIQUE!
LOOK!! OVER THERE--!
EH? WHAT? WHERE--?
I DON'T SEE ANYTHING. YOU MEAN THAT ROCK?
I'M SORRY PERCY! HE WAS GOING TO GROUND ME!
SO WHAT'S TH' BIG DEAL ABOUT LOSING A FEW WEEKENDS?
NO... HE WAS GOING TO GROUND ME INTO PASTE.

DESPITE PERCY'S BRILLIANT STRATEGY AND THEIR BRAVE VALIANT HEARTS, THE HALF-WITS ARE DRIVEN BACK!

WE'RE ALL GONNA DIE! RUN AWAY! RUN AWAY!

CLOP CLOP CLOP

YOU SEE...IT IS AS I FORETOLD!

WE'RE ALL GONNA DIE! RUN AWAY! RUN AWAY!

WILL... ...YOU... ...QUIT... ...FREAKING... ME... ...OUT?!!

BUT THE CAMPERS HAVE UNSUSPECTED ALLIES, FOR ALL THE STUFFED COWS IN THE CITY WERE BUILT BY ONE MAN...

UNCLE TOY'S BOB STORE

OPEN

Sale $1.00 ea. STUFFED COWS

Sale $2.00 FOR 2!! STUFFED COW

...DEAD-EYE GUS!!

"MOO."

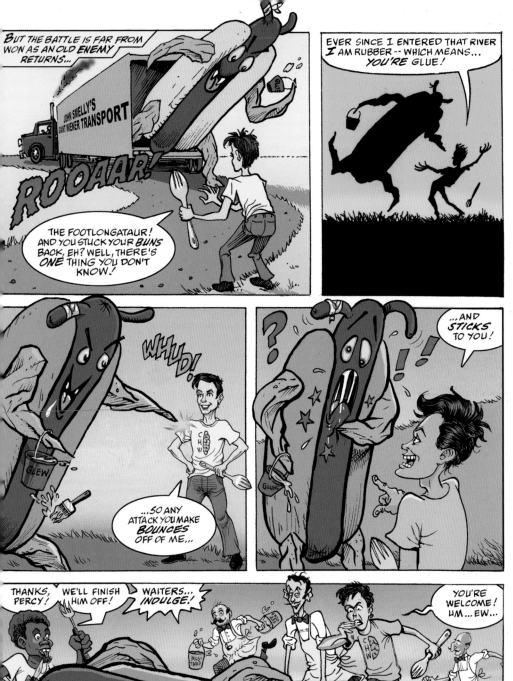

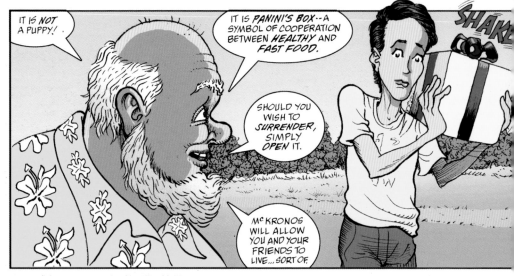

PERCY -- I KNOW WHAT'S GOING TO HAPPEN! YOU'RE *NOT* THE ONE DESTINED TO DEFEAT M^cKRONOS!

THAT'S WHAT *I* KEEP TRYING TO *TELL* HIM, BUT HE WON'T LISTEN! I OPENED UP THE BOX AND *EVERYTHING!*

I *KNOW* YOU THINK YOU'RE A GREAT *HERO* -- THAT YOU'RE SUPPOSED TO *SAVE* THE WORLD -- BUT YOU *MUST* LET *FATE* HAPPEN!

HEY, I'M *FINE* WITH IT!

DON'T TRY TO FOOL *ME!*

YOU'RE *STILL* PLANNING TO FACE M^cKRONOS --

-- EVEN IF IT MEANS SACRIFICING YOUR *LIFE!*

MY *LIFE??!!*

NO WAY!

I WOULDN'T RISK A *BRUISE.*

IN FACT, I'M *OUT* OF HERE! I WAS JUST WAITING FOR A LULL SO I COULD MAKE IT TO THE *DOOR!*

NO --!! YOU'RE TRYING TO SNEAK OUT TO FIGHT *HIM!*

HEY --!! LET *GO* --!! WHAT ARE YOU -- *PSYCHOTIC?*

YES!

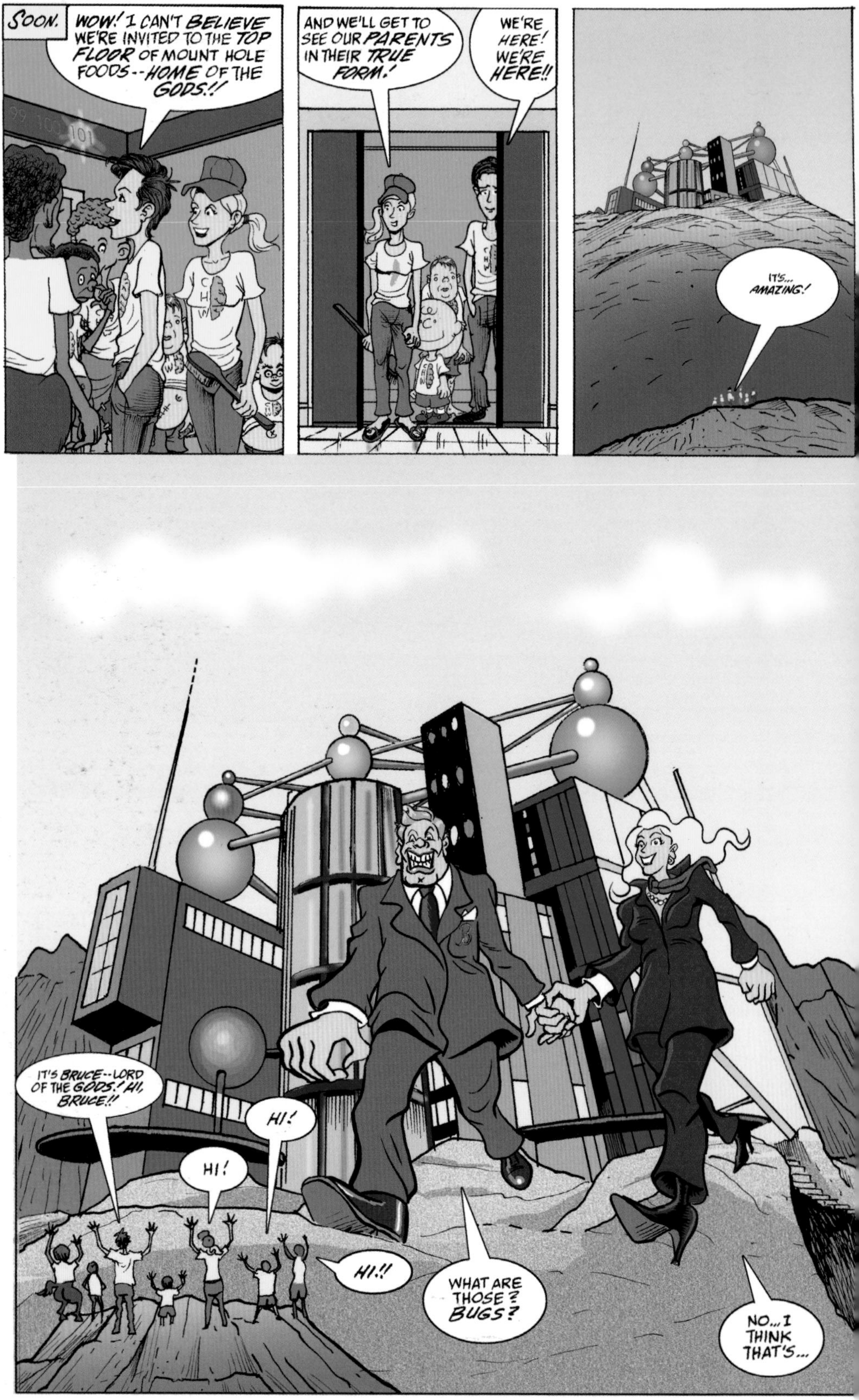
SOON.
WOW! I CAN'T BELIEVE WE'RE INVITED TO THE TOP FLOOR OF MOUNT HOLE FOODS--HOME OF THE GODS!!
AND WE'LL GET TO SEE OUR PARENTS IN THEIR TRUE FORM!
WE'RE HERE! WE'RE HERE!!
IT'S... AMAZING!
IT'S BRUCE--LORD OF THE GODS! HI, BRUCE!!
HI!
HI!
HI!!
WHAT ARE THOSE? BUGS?
NO... I THINK THAT'S...

WATCH OUT FOR PAPERCUTZ

Welcome to the time-consuming and tactless third volume of PAPERCUTZ SLICES, the semi-new graphic novel series dedicated to poking fun at your favorite pop culture phenomenon and taking no prisoners. I'm Jim Salicrup, your foolish and mostly mortal Editor-in-Chief, here to attempt and explain, and if necessary, to even apologize, while plugging other Papercutz graphic novels.

If you're just joining us, then you're very lucky! Not because you didn't have to suffer through "Harry Potty and the Deathly Boring" or "breaking down," but because you can still purchase those prize examples of unauthorized parody at either your favorite bookseller (bookstore, online bookseller, or comics shop) or directly from Papercutz (see details on page 2).

If you've already picked up the previous PAPERCUTZ SLICES, and you're still looking for graphic novels that can tickle your funny bone, and you're already up to speed on THE SMURFS graphic novels by the legendary Peyo and the GARFIELD & Co graphic novels based on Jim Davis's lasagna-loving, fat cat, then maybe it's time we tell you about the latest and greatest graphic novels heading your way from Papercutz.

First, there's the touching tale of Nina… and Sybil, the fairy who lives in her backpack. Created by Michael Rodrigue, and beautifully illustrated by Antonello Dalena and Manuela Razzi, SYBIL THE BACKPACK FAIRY explores what would happen to a middle school girl, with a younger brother, a single mom, and who is bullied at school, if she had her very own fairy. Check out the preview on the next page, to get a small taste of how much fun the series will be.

Then, even though we love all our wonderful creators equally, we're especially proud to add the world-famous Lewis Trondheim to the terrific Papercutz talent pool. His series is called MONSTER, and the first volume is called MONSTER CHRISTMAS. The series features an almost normal family and their almost ordinary adventures… and their pet monster. Check out the extra-long preview that starts in just a couple of pages!

Finally, we're offering a sneak peek as well at ERNEST & REBECCA. Rebecca is a 6 ½ year-old girl, and Ernest is her pet germ. Written by Guillamo Bianco, and illustrated by the very productive Antonello Dalena, it's another new series we suspect you'll laugh with and love! Check out the preview on our very last page.

And wait till you see what we have planned for PAPERCUTZ SLICES #4! Rather than just tell you what best-selling series we'll be spoofing next time, we'll just make a little GAME out of it. But if you really HUNGER for the answer, you'll just have to keep an eye on our website – www.papercutz.com– where you'll always find out the latest news!

So, until we meet again-- May the Farce be with you,

Jim

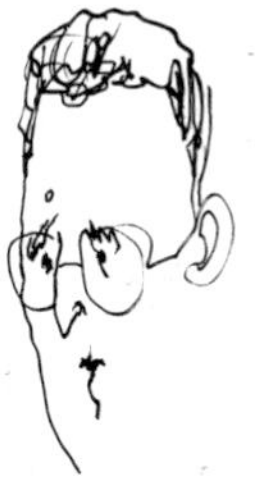

Special preview of
SYBIL THE BACKPACK FAIRY #1 "Nina"

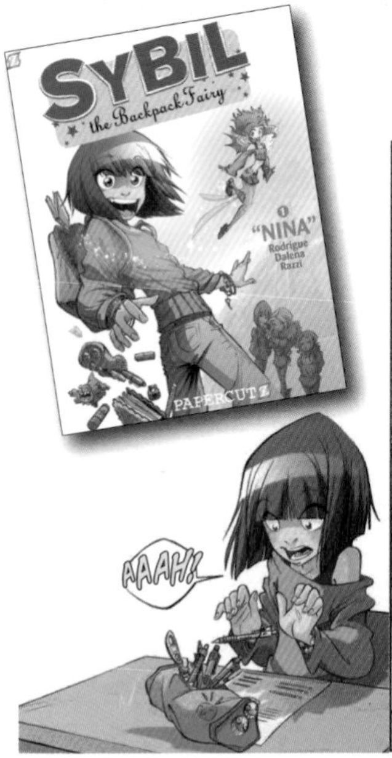
SYBIL
the Backpack Fairy
1
"NINA"
Rodrigue
Dalena
Razzi
PAPERCUTZ
AAAH!

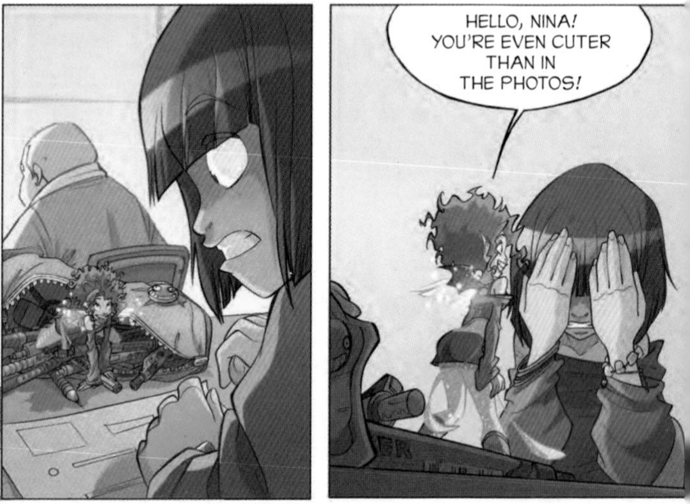
HELLO, NINA! YOU'RE EVEN CUTER THAN IN THE PHOTOS!

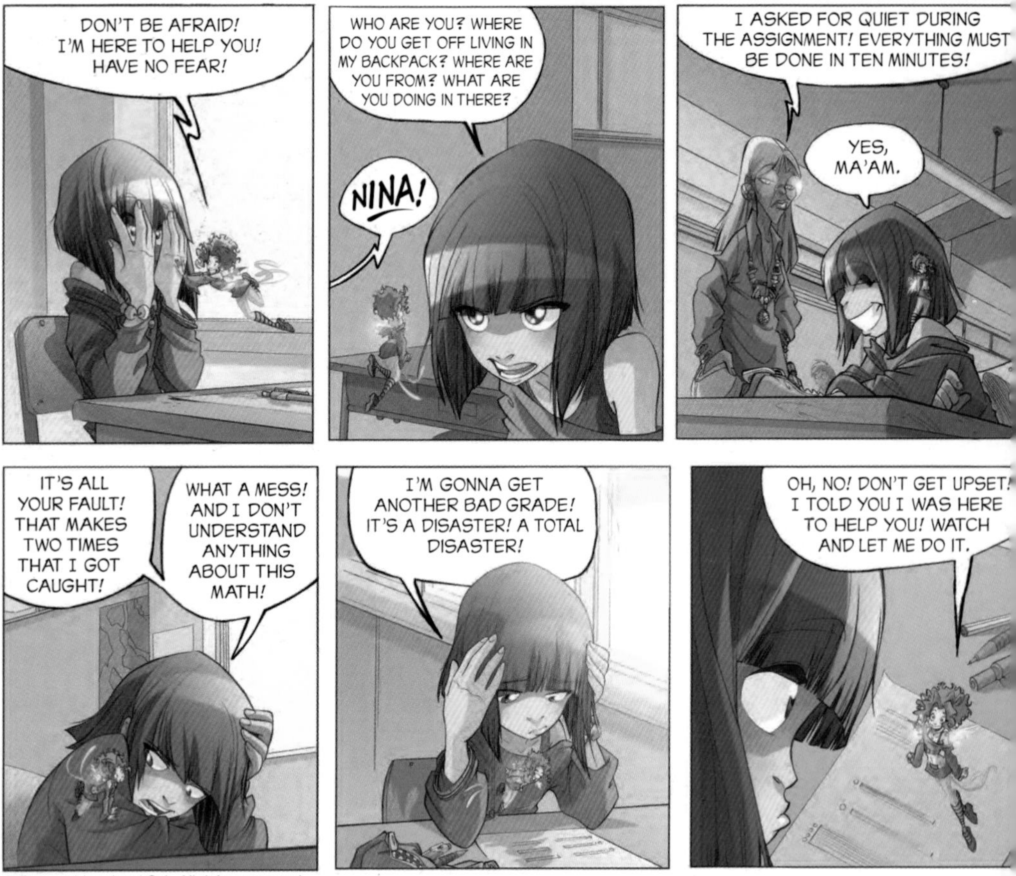
DON'T BE AFRAID! I'M HERE TO HELP YOU! HAVE NO FEAR!
WHO ARE YOU? WHERE DO YOU GET OFF LIVING IN MY BACKPACK? WHERE ARE YOU FROM? WHAT ARE YOU DOING IN THERE?
NINA!
I ASKED FOR QUIET DURING THE ASSIGNMENT! EVERYTHING MUST BE DONE IN TEN MINUTES!
YES, MA'AM.
IT'S ALL YOUR FAULT! THAT MAKES TWO TIMES THAT I GOT CAUGHT!
WHAT A MESS! AND I DON'T UNDERSTAND ANYTHING ABOUT THIS MATH!
I'M GONNA GET ANOTHER BAD GRADE! IT'S A DISASTER! A TOTAL DISASTER!
OH, NO! DON'T GET UPSET! I TOLD YOU I WAS HERE TO HELP YOU! WATCH AND LET ME DO IT.

Don't miss SYBIL THE BACKPACK FAIRY #1 "Nina"
coming November 2011!

SPECIAL PREVIEW OF MONSTER CHRISTMAS by Lewis Trondheim…

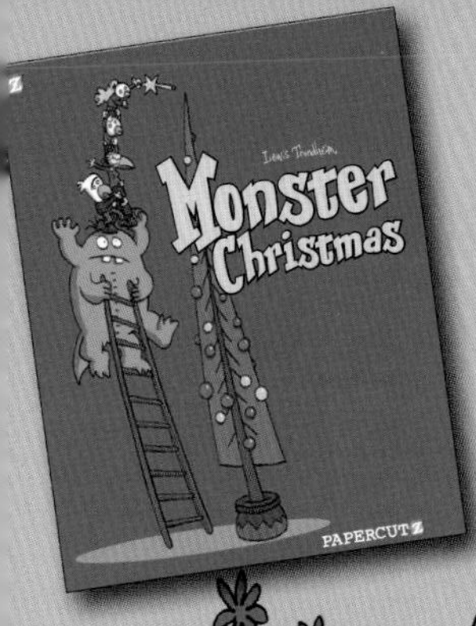
Lewis Trondheim
Monster Christmas
PAPERCUTZ

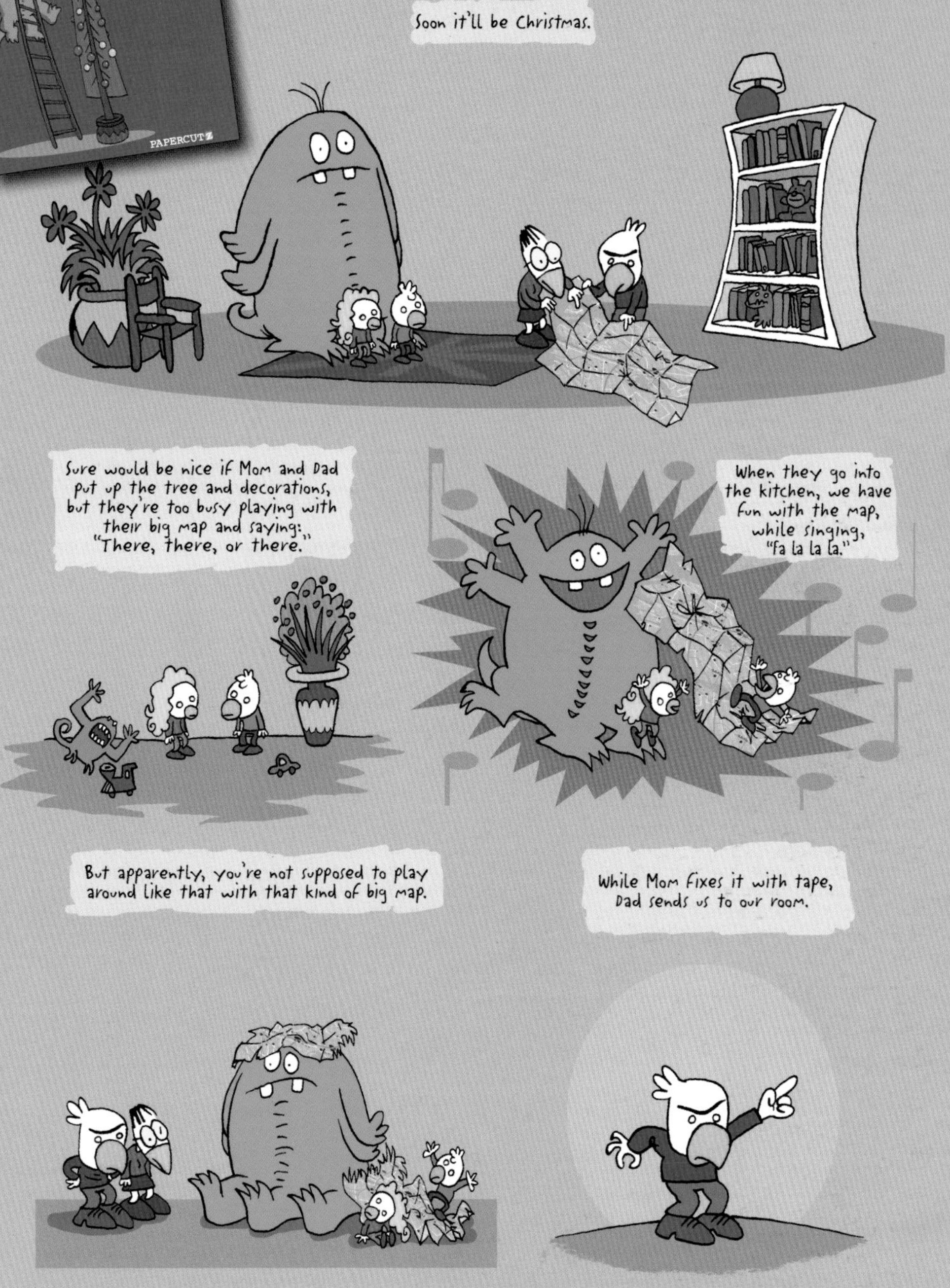
Soon it'll be Christmas.
Sure would be nice if Mom and Dad put up the tree and decorations, but they're too busy playing with their big map and saying: "There, there, or there."
When they go into the kitchen, we have fun with the map, while singing, "Fa la la la."
But apparently, you're not supposed to play around like that with that kind of big map.
While Mom fixes it with tape, Dad sends us to our room.

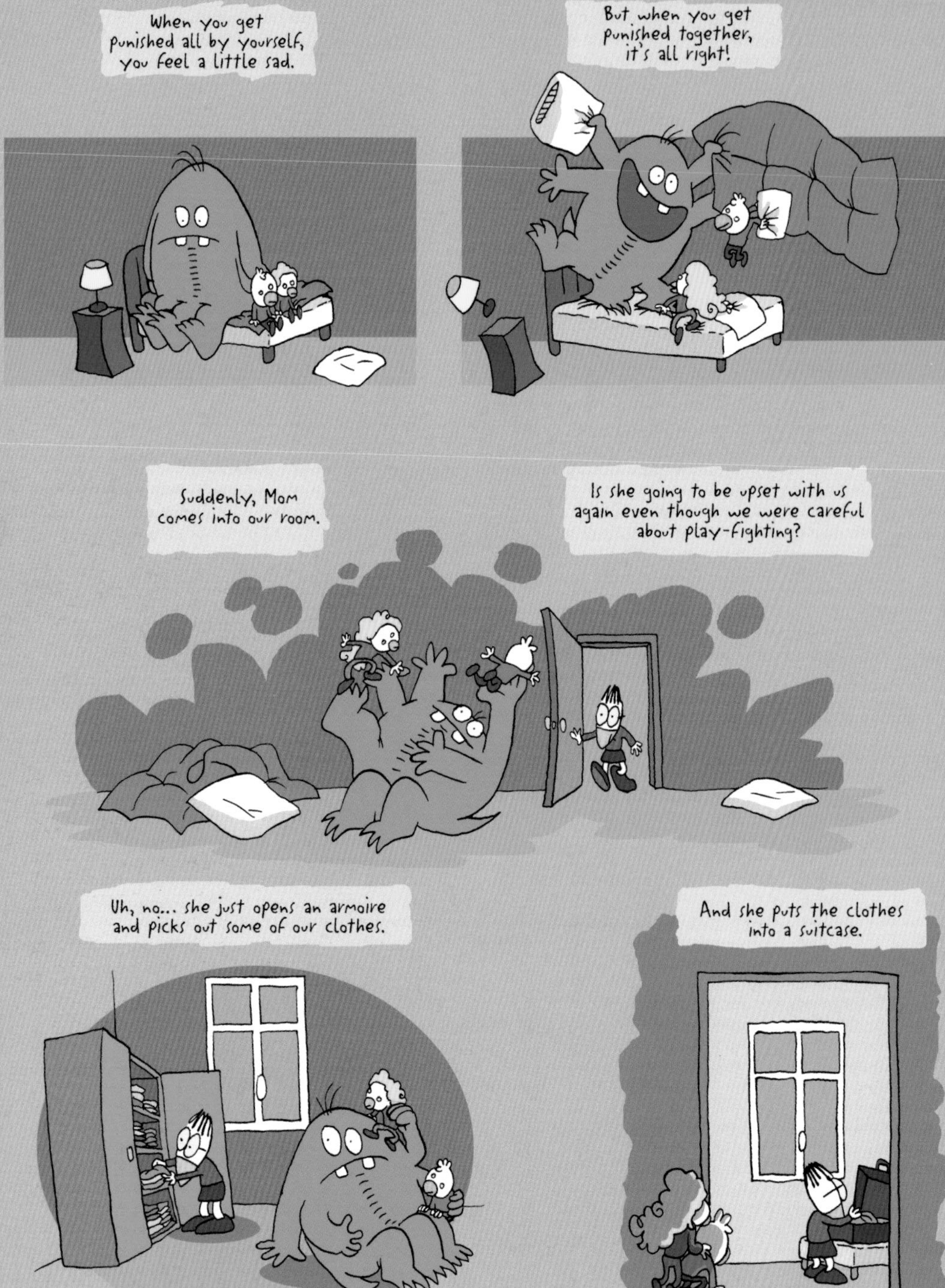
When you get punished all by yourself, you feel a little sad.
But when you get punished together, it's all right!
Suddenly, Mom comes into our room.
Is she going to be upset with us again even though we were careful about play-fighting?
Uh, no... she just opens an armoire and picks out some of our clothes.
And she puts the clothes into a suitcase.

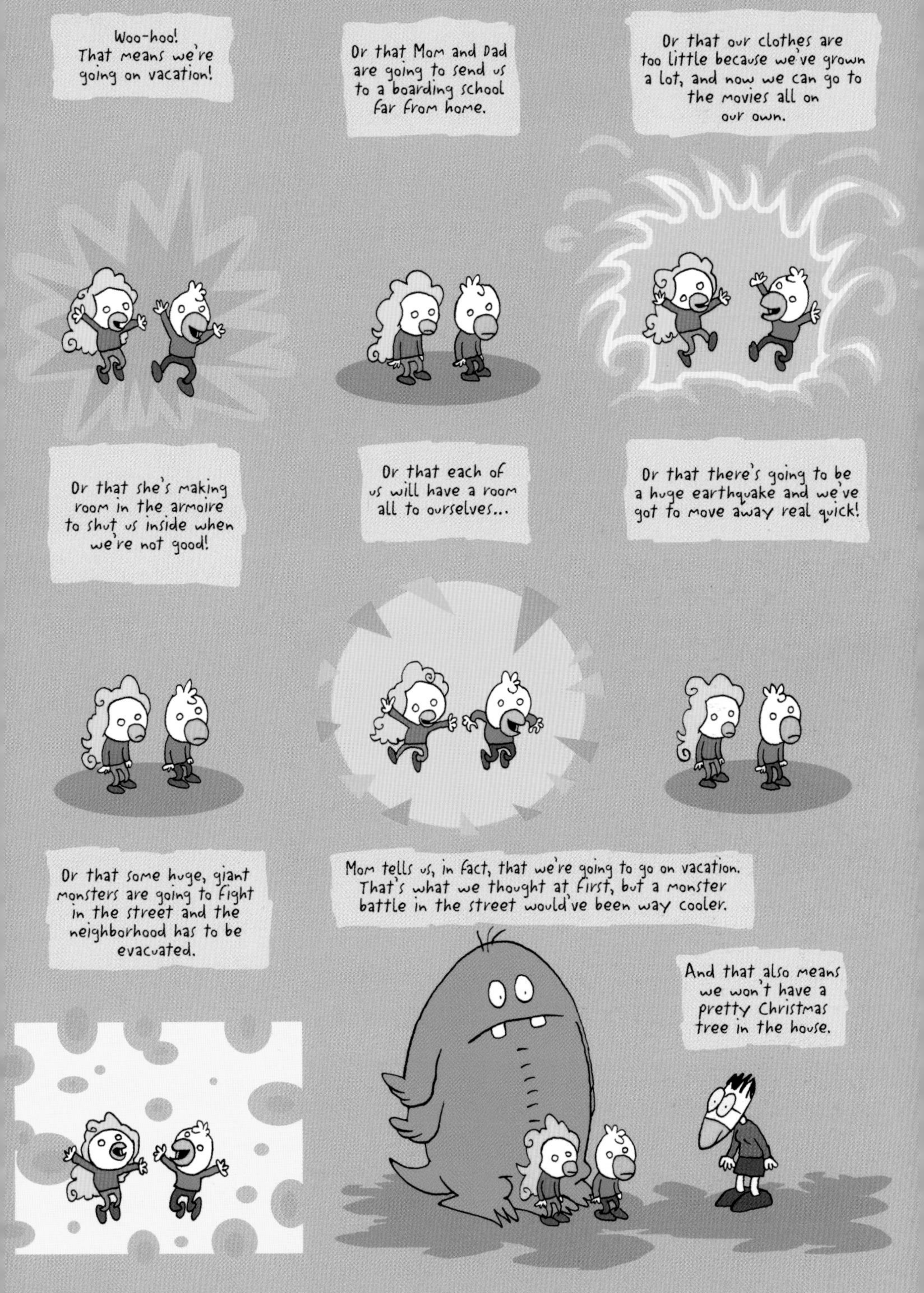
Woo-hoo! That means we're going on vacation!
Or that Mom and Dad are going to send us to a boarding school far from home.
Or that our clothes are too little because we've grown a lot, and now we can go to the movies all on our own.
Or that she's making room in the armoire to shut us inside when we're not good!
Or that each of us will have a room all to ourselves...
Or that there's going to be a huge earthquake and we've got to move away real quick!
Or that some huge, giant monsters are going to fight in the street and the neighborhood has to be evacuated.
Mom tells us, in fact, that we're going to go on vacation. That's what we thought at first, but a monster battle in the street would've been way cooler.
And that also means we won't have a pretty Christmas tree in the house.

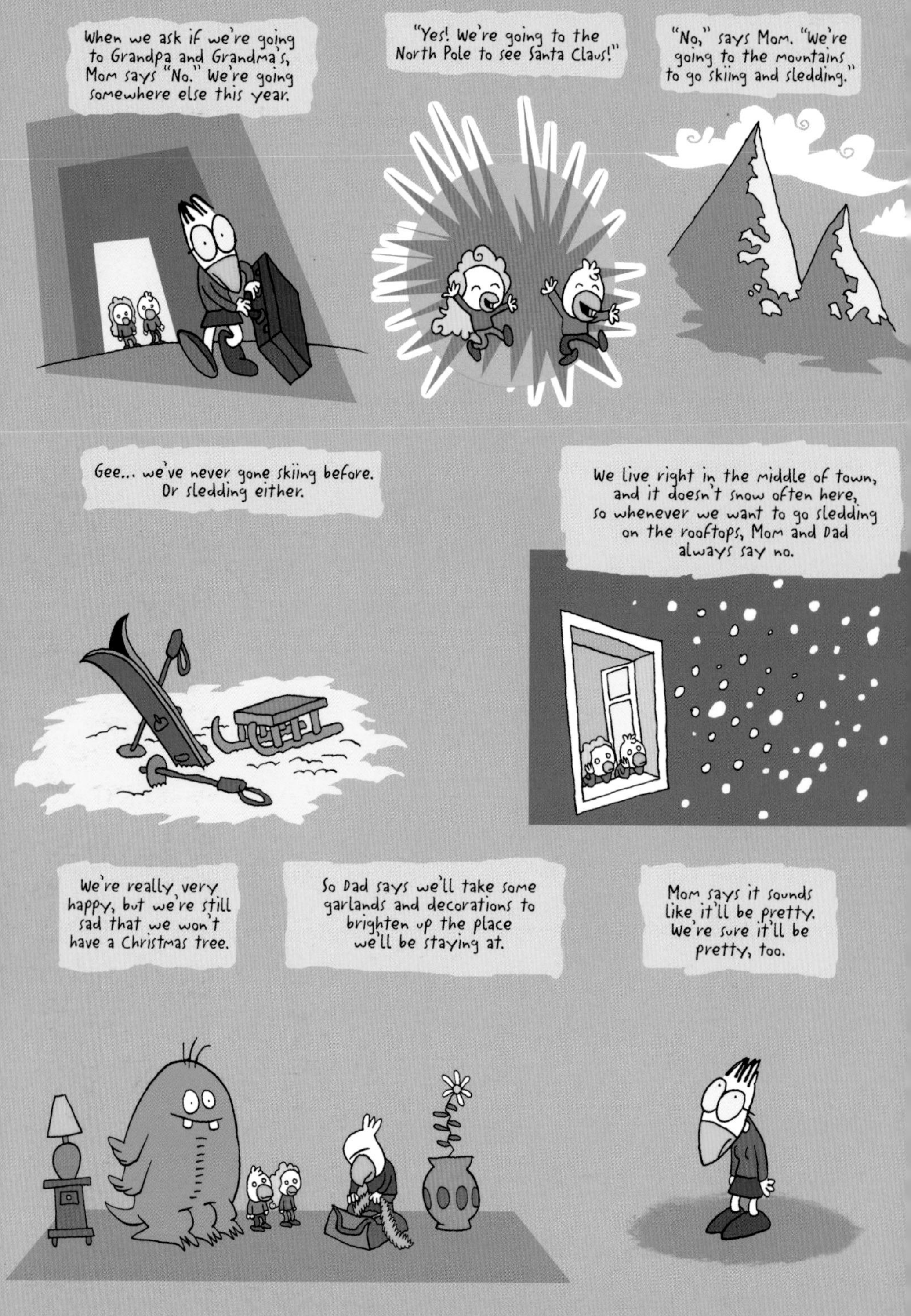
When we ask if we're going to Grandpa and Grandma's, Mom says "No." We're going somewhere else this year.
"Yes! We're going to the North Pole to see Santa Claus!"
"No," says Mom. "We're going to the mountains to go skiing and sledding."
Gee... we've never gone skiing before. Or sledding either.
We live right in the middle of town, and it doesn't snow often here, so whenever we want to go sledding on the rooftops, Mom and Dad always say no.
We're really very happy, but we're still sad that we won't have a Christmas tree.
So Dad says we'll take some garlands and decorations to brighten up the place we'll be staying at.
Mom says it sounds like it'll be pretty. We're sure it'll be pretty, too.

Mom and Dad pack the bags,
while we help by being good
and watching a DVD.

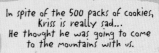

"Okay," says Dad. "Kriss, you're going
to stay home and be good.
There are 500 packs of
chocolate cookies for you
in the garage."

In spite of the 500 packs of cookies,
Kriss is really sad...
He thought he was going to come
to the mountains with us.

We tell Mom and Dad we'd like
Kriss to go with us...
Dad says that even if he wanted
Kriss to go, there wouldn't be
enough room for him in the car.

Sadly we say goodbye to Kriss and we promise
to bring him back some snowballs.
That way, we'll all have fun together
in the backyard.

Then we go peepee, because you always have to go peepee before going anywhere in the car.

Once we're in the car, we're not supposed to keep asking "Are we there yet?" That annoys Mom and Dad.

But we're kids and we ask anyways.

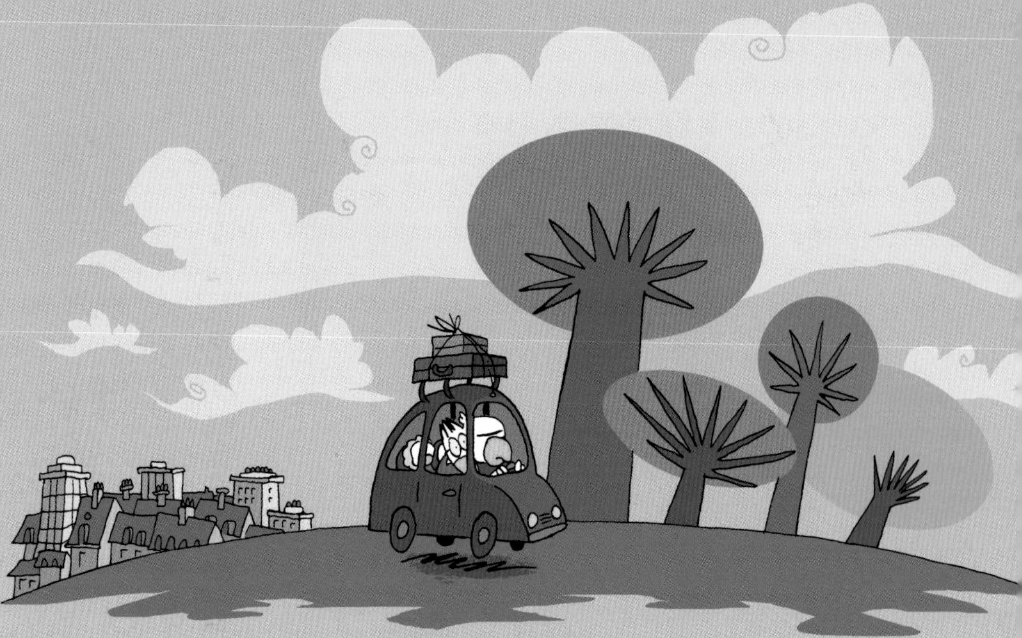

The car is nice because we're going somewhere else, but it's boring because you can't do anything in it, and what's more, we're buckled in...

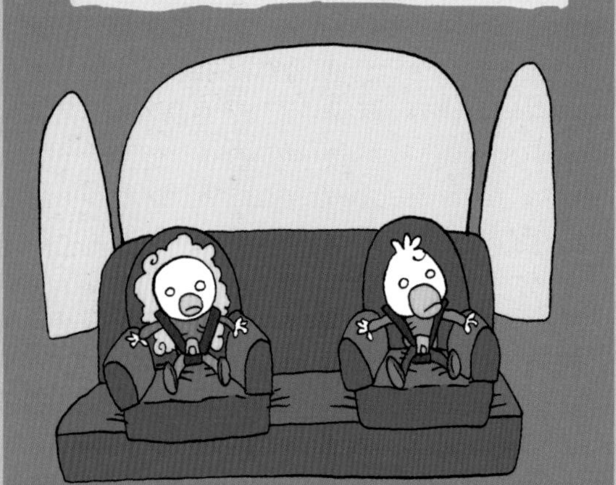

So, we ask to eat and to drink— and then, afterwards, we need to go peepee.

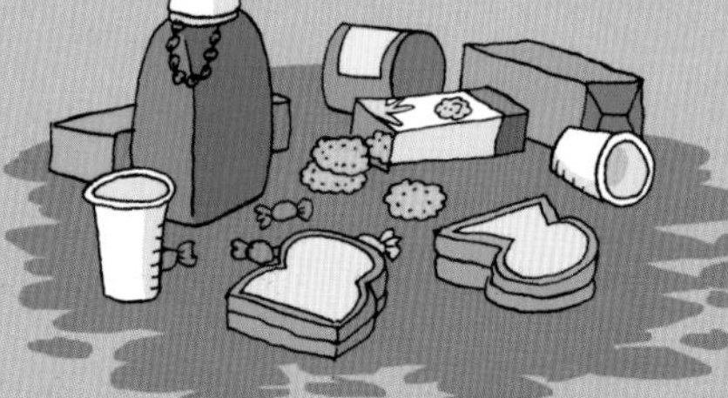

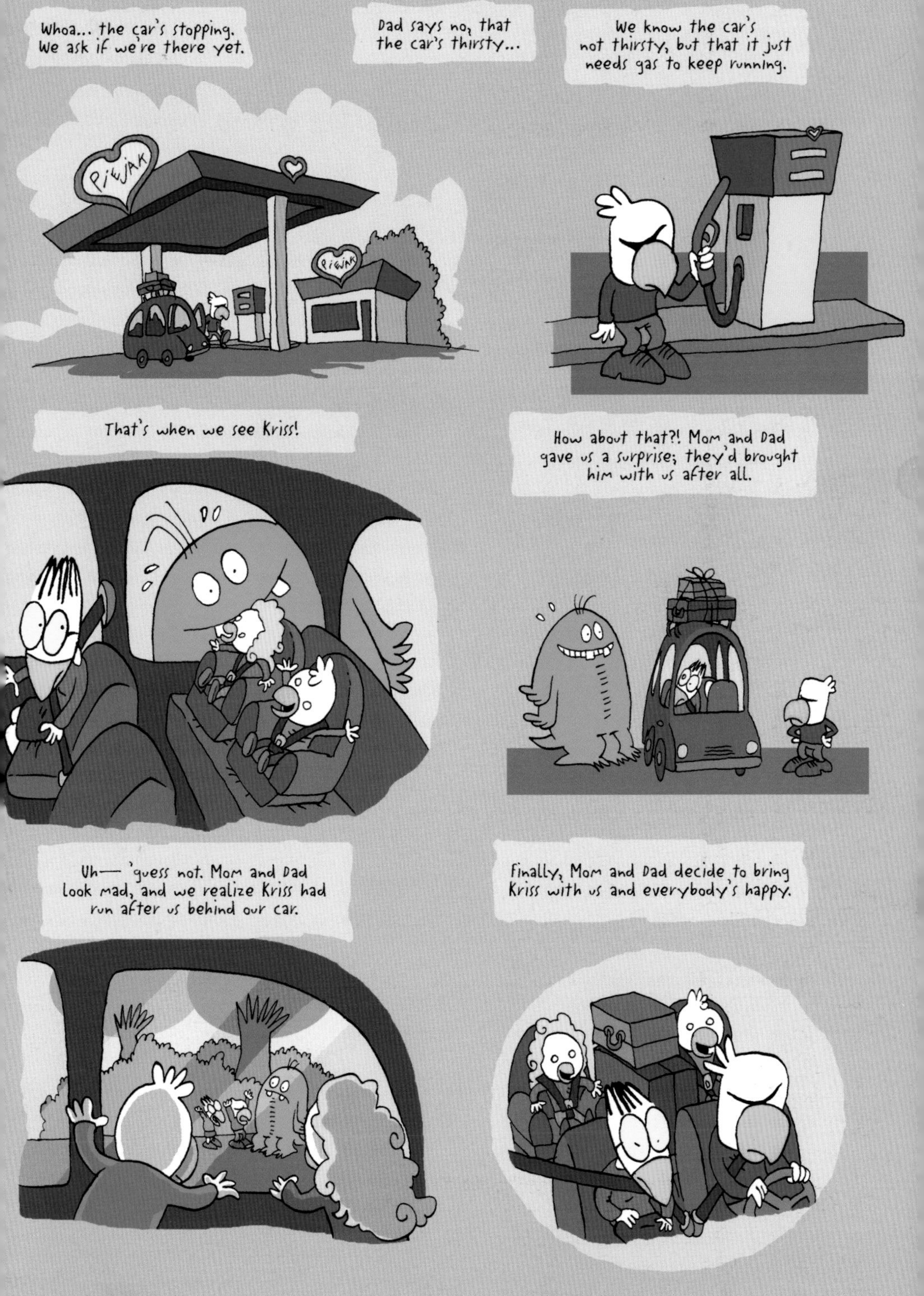
Whoa... the car's stopping. We ask if we're there yet.
Dad says no, that the car's thirsty...
We know the car's not thirsty, but that it just needs gas to keep running.
PIEJAK
PIEJAK
That's when we see Kriss!
How about that?! Mom and Dad gave us a surprise; they'd brought him with us after all.
Uh— 'guess not. Mom and Dad look mad, and we realize Kriss had run after us behind our car.
Finally, Mom and Dad decide to bring Kriss with us and everybody's happy.

Special preview of ERNEST & REBECCA #1 "My Best Friend is a Germ"

Don't miss ERNEST & REBECCA #1 "My Best Friend is a Germ"
coming November 2011!